FROZEN TROPHIES

The six men emerged into the maintenance area, and Lynch shone the light around—then stopped, pointing the beam at a drying puddle of something reddish brown. Slowly, he swung the light upward.

"Oh, my God," he said.

Schaefer frowned. "Looks as if those bastards found some time to play," he said.

Lynch moved the light along the row of corpses. To the men below it seemed to go on forever—three, five, eight . . .

Twelve dead bodies hung there—twelve *human* bodies, and to one side, two dead dogs. Crooked lines of something sparkled here and there on their sides, and hung from their heads and dangling fingertips, giving them a surreal appearance—icicles of frozen blood and sweat.

Don't miss any of these exciting *Aliens* and *Aliens vs. Predator* adventures from Bantam Books!

PREDATOR™

COLD WAR

Nathan Archer

**Based on the Dark Horse Comics graphic novel by
Mark Verheiden**

BANTAM BOOKS
NEW·YORK   TORONTO   LONDON   SYDNEY   AUCKLAND

PREDATOR: COLD WAR
A Bantam Spectra Book / May 1997

SPECTRA and the portrayal of a boxed "s" are trademarks of Bantam Books, a
division of Random House, Inc.

ISBN 0-553-57493-0

Published simultaneously in the United States and Canada

Bantam Books are published by Bantam Books, a division of Random House, Inc.
Its trademark, consisting of the words "Bantam Books" and the portrayal of a
rooster, is Registered in U.S. Patent and Trademark Office and in other countries. Marca Registrada. Bantam Books, 1540 Broadway, New York, New York
10036.

PRINTED IN THE UNITED STATES OF AMERICA
OPM 10 9 8 7 6 5 4

Dedicated to
Uncle Lew
and
Great-uncle Miles

1

Pale emptiness stretched from horizon to horizon before him. Despite the night and the heavy overcast, the world was dimly lit by reflected glow, trapped between clouds and snow; the sun would not be seen here again until the approach of spring, but there was still a faint light.

A strong wind was blowing down from the north, howling like a living thing, as if the air itself were in pain from the cold. Fine powdered snow, frozen as hard and sharp as ground glass, whipped across the icy gray desolation in bitter swirls and eddies.

Taro kept his head bent, shielding his face from the wind and cold, as he trudged across the wasteland. He didn't need to see very far to know where he was going; despite the drifting, blowing snow and the dim light, he could see the tracks of his runaway.

1

The snow was packed down by wind and frozen into ice, so that Taro walked on a surface as solid as bare ground, and his prey's tiny hooves hadn't pierced it any more than his own heavy boots did. The sharp tips, though, which had evolved to keep reindeer from skidding on the ice, had chipped at the surface here and there, and the tiny marks had caught the snow as it blew across. Miniature drifts had formed in shifting chevrons a few centimeters across, growing from the chips like crystals growing in a supersaturated solution.

At the end of the trail Taro knew he would find his missing reindeer. He suspected that he would not find it alive—a healthy animal would not have wandered off aimlessly into the taiga, leaving the herd behind, and Taro expected to find this one dead or dying.

Still, it was his duty to find it and to retrieve whatever might still be of use. If the meat was unfit to eat there would still be the hide and bone.

If he lost the trail he would turn back, and hope to stumble across the carcass on some other, warmer day.

Another man, accustomed to a warmer climate, might have worried about spoilage ruining the meat, or about pilferage, if he left the carcass for a week or two, but Taro had grown up in this Siberian wasteland, had spent his life here; nothing ever spoiled here, nothing rotted, and there was no one, no thief or predator, to steal anything. The dead could lie untouched for millennia. Mammoths found in the ice near here had still been fit to eat.

He glanced up as something caught his eye, a glimpse of movement, a flicker across the ice. He blinked and peered upward.

Something was moving across the sky above the clouds, something that glowed brightly enough to be seen faintly even through the gray overcast.

A new American plane, perhaps, testing the borders? There had been rumors for years of a craft the Americans called "Aurora" that could evade every Russian defense—but that was supposed to be invisible from the ground, flying too high and too fast to be seen.

The glow was brightening steadily, descending through the clouds and moving nearer at a fantastic speed.

It *had* to be Aurora, Taro thought; what else could move so fast? He had seen Russian planes many times, on patrol, on maneuvers, bringing in the men and equipment for the pipeline and the drilling sites and the pumping stations all along the Assyma section of the Yamal oil fields, and none of them had ever moved anywhere near so fast as this.

And then the thing burst out of the clouds in a ball of brilliant orange flame, washing the pale landscape in vivid color. It roared overhead before Taro could see it clearly; the air itself rippled visibly with the ferocity of the thing's passage.

It was *huge,* and made a sound louder than anything Taro had ever before heard, far louder than the howl of the worst storm he could remember. In its wake the air seemed warmer—but what sort of craft could warm the Siberian winter itself? That had to be an illusion, Taro told himself.

And then the thing crashed, with a boom that made the roar of its passage seem a mere whisper.

Taro turned and stared after it.

The horizon glowed orange, and again he thought he could feel heat, as if from an immense fire.

That had been unmistakably a *crash,* not a mere landing. If that had been the American Aurora spy plane, then it was down, and the authorities in Moscow would want to know—the long Cold War might be over, but that didn't mean the Russian authorities would pass up a chance to get a good close look at some top-secret American technology. The Russian government wouldn't mind a chance to score a few moral points against the Americans, either—a polite complaint about Americans spying on peace-loving post-Communist Russia might coax a few face-saving trade concessions out of somebody.

There might even be survivors, and a heroic rescue could be very good not just for Russia, but for Taro. He might be famous, might be taken to Moscow and given a medal or something. While he was reasonably content as a reindeer herder, he wouldn't mind a taste of city life, or at least a chance to pick up a few modern comforts.

If he headed back to the village and the radio there was working, he could contact the army squad stationed at the Assyma pumping station, and they could send out a truck or helicopter—but that would take three hours back, and at least an hour for the truck or copter to find the crash site.

If he headed for the site directly, though, he judged that he could reach it in an hour and a half to two hours. If there were injured survivors that extra hour or two might be crucial. If there were valuables to be salvaged, he wouldn't mind getting to them first rather than merely guiding in a bunch of soldiers.

He set out across the ice, walking straight

toward the orange glow and abandoning his hunt. His lost reindeer would keep.

In the Siberian cold *anything* would keep.

After he had been walking for a little over an hour Taro began to notice the warmth more than ever. At first he still told himself it was his imagination, that he was dreaming that cookfire heat; after all, the glow had faded away, and he was steering now by more ordinary landmarks. He couldn't really be feeling any heat from the downed aircraft, not when he was still, so far as he could judge, about two kilometers away, and when the craft had been down for so long.

Ten minutes later, though, he could no longer deny it; he was sweating in his heavy furs. He threw back his hood, and meltwater dripped down his brow.

He blinked it away and stopped in his tracks.

He was still a kilometer or so from the long, crooked ravine that cut across the icy plain, but he could see it ahead. That wasn't what troubled him; he had known the ravine was there. No, he stopped because the ice between himself and the ravine didn't look right; it glistened, not with the hard crystalline glitter it ought to have, but with a slick wet gleam.

Taro frowned, took several steps, then carefully knelt down. He put a gloved finger to the ground, then picked it up and looked at it.

The tanned leather of his glove had darkened with moisture. The ice was *wet*.

He wasn't dreaming the heat. It was real.

He didn't like that at all. A thaw in the Siberian winter? Something melting the permafrost? Even the American Aurora superplane surely couldn't generate *that* much heat!

The rifle he carried on his back was rarely used. He had it not because he really needed it, but as a mark of status among his people, a reminder that his grandfather had fought the Nazis in the Great Patriotic War. There were few predators to defend against out here on the ice, either human or beast; the stories of wolves prowling the vicinity dated mostly from his grandfather's time and might just be the lies of old men who wanted to reaffirm their own claims to manhood when they could no longer act as men.

Taro had on occasion fired the rifle in celebration, he had fired it several times in target practice, and twice to put injured reindeer out of their suffering, but he had never used it in self-defense. He had never had any need to defend himself with anything more than words or fists.

Now, though, he pulled the weapon from its fur-lined sheath and checked it over carefully. It seemed to be, as always, in perfect condition.

With the rifle ready in his arms, he advanced cautiously toward the ravine, careful of his footing on the melt-slicked ice.

The thing that had fallen from the sky in a fireball had landed *inside* the ravine ahead, he realized. He frowned. He knew that crevasse; he had lost a yearling there once. It was a long, narrow, rocky canyon; in the summer thaws it carried a trickle of meltwater north to the sea. In winter it was as dry and frozen as anywhere else, but too wide and deep for the snow to bury it completely.

The edges of the canyon were treacherous—drifted snow and built-up ice would extend out beyond the supporting rock, and a man or reindeer who got too close might well tumble in and be unable to climb back up the icy sides.

If the fallen object was down there, any investigation would be difficult. Taro frowned and slowed his pace.

Something flickered, just at the edge of his vision. He turned, startled, and brought the rifle to bear . . .

On nothing. There was nothing there, just the empty plain of ice.

Taro blinked and thought he saw a shimmer in the air somewhere to one side. He jerked the rifle over a few centimeters, thinking he must have caught a reflection on the ice—but a reflection of what?

Then a light sparkled, three moving dots of red that skittered across the ice almost too fast to follow, then skimmed up his body and settled onto his forehead, the three of them wavering about until they settled into a tidy little triangle. Taro could feel them as tiny spots of warmth, could see the red beams, but he could not make out where they were coming from, could not think what they could be. They seemed to be coming from a patch of empty air.

Then something flared blue-white, lighting the snow on all sides, and Taro knew no more.

2

Lieutenant Ligacheva was six months into her first command, and felt that she had settled in nicely. She was the lone officer in charge of the enlisted men of the little guard detachment at Pumping Station #12 on the Assyma Pipeline on the eastern fringe of the Yamal oil fields, and as such, she was responsible for making sure that the dozen pipeline workers at the station didn't go on strike, that the local reindeer herders didn't get into fights with anyone at the station, and that the Americans weren't going to invade across the polar ice. If anyone tried to sabotage the pipeline, it was her duty to make sure the attempt failed.

The men weren't interested in striking, though, nor were there any terrorists or invading Americans to be seen, and the villagers were more concerned with cadging liquor off the workers than in fighting with anyone.

Her job therefore was not particularly demanding—but then, she was a newly promoted lieutenant, and she couldn't expect anything more. She hadn't yet proven herself capable of handling duties beyond the drudgery of a routine guard post on the northern frontier.

The easy job didn't mean that she hadn't had any trouble at all, though. She was the only woman in the entire place, and when she first arrived, she had feared that that might cause problems—the old Soviet Union had paid lip service to equality of the sexes, but modern Russia didn't even do that much. A woman alone among so many men, a woman in a position of authority, could expect to encounter a certain amount of unpleasantness.

Her sex had indeed made a few difficulties at first, but she had handled them, and they were past and done. She had avoided being raped, which she had seen as the most basic part of establishing herself; she had managed it by maintaining a fierce, asexual front. To do so she had had to give up any hint of romance and remain strictly celibate, of course, but that was a price she was willing to pay for her career.

The facade had worked. As they had before her arrival, the men took any opportunity they could get to visit the accommodating, if expensive, widows in the nearby village of aboriginal reindeer herders; they left Ligacheva alone—or at any rate, they left her alone sexually. She wasn't socially isolated, thank heavens. Loneliness would be far worse than mere sexual abstinence.

She dealt with the men, both workers and

soldiers, as if she were one of them—as much as they and her rank would allow her to. There had been a few incidents, but her refusal to be offended by coarse behavior, her calm flattening of the occasional rowdy drunk, and her prowess on the soccer field behind the motor pool had established her as deserving of respect.

She was fitting in, and was pleased by it. No one tried to go around her or subvert her authority; anytime a military matter came up, she was informed. When the station's seismometers picked up a disturbance not far from the main pipe, she was summoned immediately.

She did not see at first why this disturbance concerned her—how was an earth tremor a military matter? When the messenger insisted that she had to come at once and talk to Dr. Sobchak in the little scientific station she was tempted to argue, but then she shrugged and came along; after all, now that winter had closed in and it was too cold even between storms to want to go outside, there wasn't all that much to do at Station #12. Last summer's soccer games were nothing but a fond and distant memory, and she had long since gone through everything of interest in the pumping station's tiny library. Even though she didn't like Dr. Sobchak, talking to him would at least be a break in the routine.

She did pull on her coat first, however, ignoring the messenger's fuming at the delay, and she took a certain pleasure in keeping the annoying fellow waiting while she made sure she had everything straight, the red bars on her collar perfectly aligned.

When she was satisfied she turned and marched out immediately, almost trampling the messenger, who had been caught off guard by the sudden transition.

The coat was not merely for show. The maze of tunnels that connected the station's buildings—the separate barracks for soldiers and workers, the pump room itself, the boiler plant, the extensive storerooms and equipment areas, the scientific station—was buried three meters below the snow, but was not heated; the corridors' temperature, midway between buildings, could drop well below freezing.

The lieutenant walked briskly as she strode down the tunnel, partly to maintain the proper image, but partly just to keep warm.

The scientific station was at the northernmost point of the complex; Ligacheva had plenty of time, walking through the corridors, to wonder what had Sobchak so excited. "A seismic disturbance," the messenger said—but what did that mean? Why call *her*? If there had been a quake, or an ice heave, or a subsidence, that might threaten the pipeline, but a threat to the pipeline didn't call for the army; Sobchak would have called Galyshev, the crew superintendent, to send out an inspection squad or a repair team.

And if it didn't threaten the pipeline, who *cared* about a seismic disturbance? Ligacheva had heard Sobchak explain that the instruments detected movement in the permafrost fairly often—usually during the summer thaw, of course, which was still an absolute minimum of two months away, but even in the dead of winter, so what made this one so special?

She stepped down a few centimeters from the tunnel entrance into the anteroom of the science center. The antechamber was a bare concrete box, empty save where small heaps of litter had accumulated in the corners, as cold and unwelcoming as the tunnels. Half a dozen steel doors opened off this room, but four of them, Ligacheva knew, were permanently locked—those sections of the station were abandoned. The days when the Soviet state could afford to put a dozen scientists to work out in the middle of the Siberian wilderness were long gone; Mother Russia could not spare the resources, and only Sobchak was left. The other scientists had all, one by one, been called away—to homelands that were now independent nations, to better-paid jobs in the wider world outside the old Soviet bloc, or to more important posts elsewhere in Russia, posts deserted by Ukrainians or Kazakhs or Lithuanians, or by mercenaries selling their talents abroad.

Only Sobchak was left.

The official story behind keeping Sobchak was that Russia's oil company did need *one* scientist, one geologist, to remain here to monitor the equipment that watched over the pipeline, but the lieutenant suspected that the truth was that no one else wanted Sobchak. The little man with the thick glasses and ugly mustache was sloppy, pompous, vain, and aggravating, and Ligacheva wasn't especially convinced that he had any great abilities as a scientist, either.

She opened the door to the geological monitoring station, and warm air rushed out at her—Sobchak kept his tiny kingdom as warm as he could, and old orders giving the scientists priority on the steam output from the boiler plant had never been rescinded, so that was quite warm indeed.

The geologist's workroom was good-sized, but so jammed with machinery that there was almost no space to move about. Exactly in the center sat little Sobchak, perched on his swivel chair, surrounded by his equipment—meters and displays, switches and dials on every side. He looked up at her; the fear on his face was so exaggerated that Ligacheva almost laughed. His beady little eyes, wide with terror, were magnified by his glasses; his scraggly attempt at a mustache accentuated the trembling of his upper lip. His narrow jaw and weak chin had never looked any worse.

"Lieutenant Ligacheva!" he called. "I'm glad you're here. Come look at this!"

Ligacheva stepped down the narrow space between a file cabinet and an equipment console to see where Sobchak was pointing. It was a paper chart, unscrolling from one drum and winding onto another. A pen had drawn a graph across it, a graph that had suddenly spiked upward not long ago, and was now hovering well above where it had begun.

"This is your record of seismic activity?" Ligacheva asked, unimpressed.

Sobchak looked up at her, startled. "*Seismic* activity? Oh, no, no," he said. "That's over there." He pointed to a large bank of machinery on the other side of the room, then turned back to the first chart and tapped it. "This chart shows *radiation* levels."

Ligacheva blinked at him. "What?"

"Radiation," Sobchak said. "Radioactivity."

Ligacheva stared. "What are you talking about?" she demanded.

"*This,*" Sobchak said, pointing. "This, Lieutenant. I don't know what it is. What I do know is that something happened that made the ground shake about twenty kilometers northeast of here, and that when it did there came this burst of radioactivity. Ever since then the background radiation has been four times what it should be."

"Four times, you say," Ligacheva said, fingering the paper chart.

"Yes," Sobchak said. "Four times."

"And you want me and my men to go find out what this thing is, that's radiating like this."

"*Yes,*" Sobchak repeated.

Ligacheva stared at the chart.

It might be dangerous, whatever was out there. She didn't know what it was, and all her guesses seemed wild—an American attack? A fallen satellite?

Whatever it was, it was not any part of the established routine.

Perhaps she should report it to Moscow and await orders, but to report it when it was still just readings from old equipment that the authorities would say could not be trusted would be asking to be ignored. Sobchak's pay still came through, but Ligacheva knew that no one in power thought much of the little geologist, and as for Moscow's opinion of herself—well, if you were a general in Moscow, you didn't send a young officer out to the middle of the Yamal Peninsula because you wanted to pay close attention to her and encourage her career. General Ponomarenko, who had assigned her here, had never done anything to make her believe he respected her opinions.

If she took her men out there and they saw whatever it was with their own eyes, though, that would be harder to ignore. No one could say that the phenomenon was the result of Sobchak's imagination or of poorly maintained monitoring equipment if she had half a dozen eyewitnesses confirming . . . whatever it was out there.

She knew that no one advanced quickly in any army, let alone in the new, post-Soviet Russian Army, by staying timidly in the barracks waiting for her superiors to tell her what to do.

"Right," she said. "Where is this mysterious radioactive disturbance, exactly?"

3

The temperature out there is thirty-four degrees below zero, and it's snowing again," Salnikov said as he straightened his gunbelt and reached for his hat. "That weather is *just* right for a pleasant little twenty-kilometer stroll, don't you think so, Dmitri?"

Dolzhikov snorted. "Oh, *yes*, Pyotr, just delightful," he said as he yanked on his second boot. "I'm *so* pleased we're all being sent out on this little errand!" He stamped the boot into place. "I wonder, though, Pyotr, if perhaps our beloved Sobchak's instruments would be just ever so slightly less sensitive if *he* were the one sent to investigate every little knock and tumble."

"That's not fair, Dmitri," Utkin said mildly, looking up from checking the action on his AK-74. "How many times before has Sobchak sent us out now? Two, maybe three, in the past year?"

"And how many times have we found anything?" Dolzhikov retorted as he rose from his bunk and reached for his overcoat. "Last time, as I recall, a reindeer had tripped over one of Sobchak's seismographs. How *very* important it must have been to investigate that and report every detail to Moscow at once!"

"Now, Dmitri," Salnikov said, grinning. "That might have been an American reindeer, spying on us!" He clapped his gloved hands together. "Besides, is it Sobchak who sends us out, or is it the bold Lieutenant Ligacheva?"

"At least the lieutenant comes with us," Dolzhikov muttered, fumbling with his buttons, "while Sobchak stays huddled in his little laboratory, watching all the gauges on his precious machines."

"Watching the gauges is Sobchak's job," Lieutenant Ligacheva barked from the doorway. "Sometimes finding out what the readings mean is yours. Now stop your griping and move! Get out to the truck!"

Utkin and Salnikov charged out the door to the waiting snow truck while the other men hurried to get the last few straps and buttons fastened; Ligacheva watched them from the doorway, settling her snow goggles into place so the others could not read her eyes.

The men had no idea why they were going out on the ice, what made this particular tremor any more worthy of investigation than any other. They could hardly be expected not to grumble, under the circumstances.

Ligacheva knew that, and saw no reason to change the circumstances. She could live with grumbling. She hadn't told the men anything about the radioactivity because she saw no need to frighten them. These were not experienced warriors who could put fear aside or who would be hardened by it; they were mostly children, boys of eighteen or nineteen with only a few weeks of arctic weather training among them all and with no knowledge of science at all. Better, she thought, to let them grumble than to panic them.

Just children—with the bold Lieutenant Ligacheva to lead them across the ice, she thought bitterly. *She* was no child, yet she was out here, too, her career as frozen as the ground around her.

She could still remember what General Ponomarenko had said the day he assigned her to the Assyma oil field. "This is an important duty, Ligacheva," he said. "Do well and there may be a place for you on my staff."

She could still remember his condescending smirk as he said it. A place on his staff, indeed. And perhaps she could grow oranges in her spare time here.

Ponomarenko had known where he was sending her—out of the way, where failure could be hidden or ignored. Such faith he had in her, sending her somewhere no one would blame him if she fouled up! And all the while he was undoubtedly patting himself on the back for his enlightened policies, for not openly trying to ruin her just because she was a woman and an outspoken democrat.

"Come on," she called to the men. "The snow won't let up for hours, and the temperature's still dropping. The longer you wait the worse it'll be, and the sooner we get this over with the sooner you'll get back to your cards and liquor."

The men came and clambered onto the "truck"—an oversized tractor on snow treads, hauling a personnel carrier. Salnikov was in the driver's seat, with the engine running; as soon as the last boot left the ice he put the tractor in gear, and the ungainly vehicle lurched forward.

Ligacheva sat silently beside him as they headed out of the pumping station complex, out to the pipeline. As they approached the immense pipe Salnikov looked at her for confirmation of their direction. She pointed. He nodded, and turned the vehicle northward. From that point on the tractor chugged steadily along the service road beside the pipeline—not the shortest route to their intended destination, but the path that would be least likely to get them lost in the arctic night.

There were just the two of them in the cab; the others all rode in the trailer, no doubt exchanging jokes and bawdy stories. Ligacheva would be surprised if no one had managed to smuggle in a liter of vodka; she imagined they'd be passing that around, giving no thought to their commander and the driver up front.

Ligacheva looked out at the swirling snow and the cold darkness beyond, at the looming concrete and steel barrier of the pipeline that blocked out half the world, all of it white and gray, devoid of color, just shapes picked out in the glare of the tractor's headlights. She felt the fierce cold beginning to seep into the cab with her and Salnikov, despite the desperate blowing of the heater.

Out here on the ice the grandstanding and maneuvers of generals and bureaucrats and politicians

back in Moscow all seemed a distant, stupid, point-
less game. Reputation didn't matter. Power didn't
matter. Staying warm, staying alive, *that* was what
mattered.

"Here," she said as the eighteen-kilometer
marker came into view, the sign on the pipeline a
sudden spot of red in the black, white, and gray
wilderness outside. "Turn east. Four kilometers."
She tapped the map she held on her knee, then
pointed to the dashboard compass. "Four kilometers," she repeated.

Salnikov looked at the map, then at the external
thermometer. He hesitated, peering out into the
empty darkness to the east.

"It . . . it's getting colder, Lieutenant," he said
uncertainly. "Forty below zero, and the snow is
heavier. Perhaps we should head back, try again
later . . ."

"It's just four kilometers farther, Salnikov,"
Ligacheva said, keeping her annoyance out of her
voice. "That's nothing. Enjoy the fresh air."

Salnikov bit back a reply and turned the tractor,
away from the comforting solidity of the pipeline
and into the unrelieved gloom of the Siberian
wilderness. When he had, Ligacheva reached down
into her pack and pulled out something she would
have preferred not to have needed.

"What's that?" Salnikov asked, glancing at the
device she held.

"Just drive," Ligacheva said. There was no need
to tell him yet that it was a Geiger counter.

It buzzed briefly when she directed the probe
ahead, but the radiation level was not dangerous
yet. In fact, Ligacheva judged it was only a little

higher than normal. Perhaps whatever had caused that spike on Sobchak's graph was gone now.

She glanced at the thermometer outside Salnikov's window. Forty-two below.

In extreme cold, she had heard, engine steel turned brittle and could snap like balsa wood. More than eighteen kilometers from the station, in snow and darkness and extreme cold—if they lost the tractor out here, most of them, maybe all of them, would die before they could get back to shelter.

She frowned at the thought, but said nothing. The engine temperature gauge was still in the normal operating range, despite the cold outside.

A few minutes later she glanced at the outside thermometer again. What she saw caught her gaze, and she stared intently, trying to understand it.

Twenty-eight below. But just a kilometer or two back it had been forty-two below.

How could it be so much warmer here?

She lifted the Geiger counter and aimed the probe. The machine crackled, the needle on its gauge jumping slightly before settling down. There was radioactivity here, more than normal—but far below dangerous levels. The stolen cigarettes she had smoked as a girl had probably been more of a long-term risk.

Still, why was there anything more than the usual background radiation?

"Lieutenant!" Salnikov cried, and his voice sounded strained and unnatural. Ligacheva looked up, through the windshield, as the wiper cleared away the latest smear of snow, and saw what had triggered Salnikov's exclamation.

"*Bozhe moi*," she said. "Oh, my God."

They were nearing the top of a low ridge. Ahead

of them in the headlight beams, on the ridgetop, a broad patch of snow shone a vivid red; a sprinkle of snowflakes had powdered it with white, but the red still showed up, shockingly bright. Above the red patch dangled a dark shape, swaying in the wind, speckled white with snow.

"Stop the truck!" Ligacheva ordered—unnecessarily; Salnikov had already shifted into neutral. "Keep the engine running," she said. If the engine were shut down, they might never get it started again out here.

The cold hit her like a gigantic wave, sucking the warmth and life out of her, as she unlatched the door of the tractor and climbed out. She shivered involuntarily as her body struggled to adjust. The wind howled in her ears, as loud as the steady rumble of the tractor's engine—no, she corrected herself, louder.

Behind her the men were jumping down from the trailer, guns in their hands.

"Wait," she called, holding up a hand. She drew her own side arm—the heft of the 9mm was comforting.

Salnikov had climbed out the other side of the cab, inching forward into the pool of light from the headlights, his AK-74 in his hands. Ligacheva didn't stop him; when he glanced over at her she motioned him forward.

A splintered pole rose from the ice at a steep angle, reaching a height of maybe three meters above the very peak of the rise; the dark, swaying shape was tied near the top of the pole, dangling there in the night.

The shape was a man's body, suspended by a rope

lashed around both ankles; his outstretched arms hung straight down, fingertips brushing the snow.

His head was gone. Where his head should have been was a thin, dark icicle of frozen blood. Below him lay a broad pool of the same substance.

Salnikov stared at the corpse for a moment, then down at the frozen pool, then at the snow around it.

"Footprints," he said. "Footprints everywhere, Lieutenant. Big ones, see?" Then he looked up at the corpse again.

"What *happened* here?" he wailed.

Ligacheva didn't answer directly—she couldn't. The only answer she could give would have been "I don't know," and she couldn't say that in front of her men, not yet.

"Who is it?" she asked. "Anyone know?"

"One of the villagers," Utkin replied. "Look at his clothes."

Ligacheva looked at the dead man's clothes—she realized she had been staring at the frozen blood, the headlights making the pool glisten like smoldering coals on the snow, rather than at the victim. Sure enough, the corpse wore the reindeer-hide garments of the local tribesmen.

"Which?" she asked. "Who is it?" She wondered whether this might be some tribal ritual she had never heard of, some frenzied rite or primitive custom, a formal vengeance, perhaps, or a sacrifice to whatever brutal arctic deities the locals might worship.

"Taro," Salnikov said.

"How can you tell?" Dolzhikov said, his voice cracking. "His head is gone!"

"His rifle is there," Salnikov said. He gestured.

"That's Taro's rifle. He was very proud of it, never let anyone else carry it."

Sure enough, a fine old hunting rifle lay half-buried in the snow behind the corpse; Ligacheva had not seen it until Salnikov pointed it out.

That eliminated the possibility that any sane human being had done this, Ligacheva thought. No one but a madman would have left so valuable an item out there in the snow.

A madman . . . then this was no tribal ritual but merely berserk slaughter.

"Footprints?" she asked Salnikov.

He nodded. "Hundreds of them." He looked around, then said, "They go that way." He hesitated. "And, Lieutenant," he added, "I have never seen such footprints. They're too big. And there are other marks, in front of every print, as if something had clawed at the snow."

"Perhaps something did. Do you mean it was a beast that did this? A beast that ties knots?"

Salnikov shook his head. "No, these are boot marks, or shoe marks—but there are claw marks *with* them, as if there were claws that stuck out the front of each boot."

"More likely the killer had some sort of trained animal," Ligacheva said. "Follow them. And be ready—whoever, or *whatever,* did this is dangerous." She waved to the others. "Utkin, Vetrov, you go with him. If you see anything move, anything strange, fire twice—don't take chances."

Utkin and Vetrov nodded and followed Salnikov reluctantly as Ligacheva called, "The rest of you, help me cut him down. We'll take him back to his people."

The pole was firmly fixed in the ice, and none of

the men could reach high enough to untie the ropes from its peak; instead two men held Taro's frozen corpse to keep it still while a third sawed through the bindings with his knife.

It took longer than Ligacheva would have thought; she resisted the urge to order Kazaryan, the knife-wielder, to hurry. The blade was probably brittle with cold; hurrying might snap it. She shivered and glanced after Salnikov and the others.

They had moved on down the slope to the east, following the trail; the wind carried away their words, and Ligacheva could not hear them as they shouted to one another.

"Look how big these prints are!" Utkin said. "Whoever made them must be a giant!"

Vetrov knelt by the trail and shook his head. "Look again," he said. "The ice melted with each step, then refroze—that's why they're so big."

Utkin stared at him. "Do you have any idea what kind of heat that would take?" He looked at Salnikov, who had moved on ahead, then turned back to Vetrov. "Besides, they must have been huge even without the melting—look at them!"

Vetrov shrugged. "Maybe," he admitted.

"The trail goes on past that next rise," Salnikov called back to them. "Perhaps from the top we can see something. Come on!"

Reluctantly the others followed, struggling up the next slope—it wasn't steep, or particularly high, but the wind was against them.

"We should have brought a light," Vetrov muttered.

"Yes," Utkin agreed. "I would like to see these footprints more clearly. I do not think anything could have melted the ice as you suppose."

"Feel them for yourself," Vetrov retorted. "The bottom of each print is slick ice."

Utkin stooped and did as Vetrov suggested. "Maybe," he conceded. "But I do not think that was what made them so large, Igor. I think it *is* a giant that we follow."

"Come on, you two," Salnikov called as he struggled up onto the top of the little rise—it wasn't really much more than an overgrown snowdrift, but it did provide a slightly elevated vantage point.

Salnikov paused, peering out into the gloom. He did not say so, but he, like Vetrov, wished they had brought a light. The night here was not utterly black, not with the clouds and snow to reflect and multiply every slightest glimmer of light, but he still could not see far through the swirling snow and the midwinter gloom.

At least, at any distance he could not be certain what he was seeing. A jagged black gap in the snow cover ahead might be a ravine or merely a shadow; he couldn't be sure. He stared, but still couldn't decide whether the canyon he thought he saw was really there.

He was sweating, he realized abruptly. His face was damp with perspiration and wasn't freezing.

He pulled off his hat and crumpled it in one hand. No ice crunched, no snow fell; instead he could see the fur was damp.

"My God," he said. "You two, can you feel it? The heat?" He stared into the darkness. Where was the warmth coming from? He saw no lights, no fires.

He could feel the heat, though—and something else.

"Something's out here," he said. "Something . . . I can feel it . . ."

His vision seemed suddenly distorted, even more than the snow, the night, and the wind could account for.

"What . . ." he began.

Then he screamed and fell backward, sliding down the icy slope.

Vetrov and Utkin had been crouched over the footprints as they advanced, not really listening to Salnikov; now they looked up just in time to catch him as he tumbled into their arms.

"Pyotr!" Utkin cried. "What . . ." He felt something warm and wet leaking into his heavy gloves.

"Look at his face!" Vetrov said.

Utkin looked.

Two parallel slashes had cut Salnikov's face open, slicing from cheekbone to throat, laying the flesh open right down to the bone—and in fact, Utkin could see a notch in the cheekbone itself, a notch that vanished beneath welling blood. Blood was spilling from Salnikov's ruined face across Utkin's hands—that was the warmth he had felt.

"What could have . . ." Utkin began, looking out past the top of the rise.

He saw only a flicker as the blade came down at him.

Vetrov had time to scream.

Once.

4

They had Taro's frozen body loaded halfway onto the truck when Lieutenant Ligacheva heard the scream. It was faint and distant, muffled by the wind, but there was no mistaking it for anything but the scream of pain it was.

"What in the . . ." She looked up in time to see something flare blue-white in the darkness beyond the ridge. "Pyotr!" she cried.

Then she remembered where she was, who she was, and who was with her.

"All of you," she barked, "follow me! Now!"

Dolzhikov hesitated, holding Taro's legs.

"Forget him!" Ligacheva shouted. "We can tend to him later!"

Dolzhikov obeyed and dropped his burden; the frozen corpse teetered, then rolled slowly out of the truck and onto the ice. Dolzhikov joined the others as they charged up the ridge, past the pole.

Ligacheva was shouting orders as she ran. "As soon as we reach Salnikov and the others, take up defensive positions! Use the ridge and the drifts for cover, if you can! No firing until I give the order!" That last was an afterthought; she didn't want anyone accidentally shooting Salnikov or Utkin or Vetrov if they were still alive out there in the dark.

She tried to imagine what could have happened, what the three men could have found, what could have left those huge footprints and the strange scratchy marks. There had only been the single trail leading away from the pole, yet she had not heard any of her men fire their weapons, and no single lunatic could have defeated them all before they could shoot—did Taro's murderer have companions? Was there an entire company of madmen waiting for them? Was this some insane invasion by Americans, or a terrorist attack by some extremist faction—Chechens, or Georgians, or Jews? Thoughts and images tumbled through her mind too quickly to make sense of any of them, to choose any as more likely.

And then Starostin's head blew off.

Ligacheva staggered and stared.

One moment Private Anton Mikhailovich Starostin had been running up the ridge beside her, eyes bright with excitement, with anticipation of his first taste of battle, and the next moment there was a blue-white flash and Starostin's head was gone, just—*gone*. The light had flashed through tissue and bone as if they weren't there. Starostin's body ran another half step and then collapsed in the snow, blood spattering across the white ground.

But there was no enemy, nothing to shoot at. The white flash had come out of nowhere.

"Where are they?" Dolzhikov cried.

"Fire if you see them!" Ligacheva shouted back.

Then the white light flashed again, and Dolzhikov was gone, his chest blown apart, one arm vanished, head flung back at a hideous, broken angle.

"We can't fight this!" someone called—Ligacheva didn't see whom and didn't recognize the voice over the howling of the wind and the incoherent shouting of her panicking troops. She turned to see someone running for the truck. "We've got to get back to the . . ."

And then the light blazed again, but this time it did not shear through flesh; instead it struck the tractor's engine compartment, and the vehicle exploded into flame.

Ligacheva knew then that she was going to die, they were *all* going to die—but she still didn't know why or who was responsible.

She wanted to know—but more than that, she wanted to take some of them with her. She snatched up Dolzhikov's AK-74 and released the safety—he hadn't even had time to do that before dying.

Ligacheva couldn't see the enemy, couldn't see her own men, but she knew it didn't matter anymore. Her men were as good as dead, with the enemy out there somewhere in the Siberian night; she opened fire, spraying steel-jacketed lead into the darkness, in the general direction the blue-white fire had come from.

Fire came again as her foot slipped on the ice and she began to tumble. White light and searing heat tore through her shoulder, and the AK-74 went flying in one direction as she fell in the other.

Snow gave beneath her, and she rolled down

the ridge; the world wheeled madly about her, a chaos of snow and cold and darkness and light, the hot orange flashes of guns and the cold white flare of the enemy's weapon, until she landed hard on wind-scoured ice, her own wind knocked out of her. Snow tumbled down upon her, almost burying her; one eye peered out through her goggles, while the lens protecting the other was covered by blank whiteness.

She was dazed, stunned by impact, by the shock of her shoulder wound, by the bitter cold that seeped through her heavy coat and down the back of her neck. She lay for a moment, unable to think or move, as the violence around her died away until the only screaming was the wind, until nothing flashed or blazed. The truck was burning, there before her—she could just see it at the edge of her field of vision—but it had settled down to a slow, steady glow, no more explosions or flare-ups. The fire's glow lit the icy landscape a hellish red-orange, giving her light to see.

Only one of her squad was in sight, lying motionless on his belly on the ice near the truck— she couldn't tell if he was alive or dead. Feigning death, perhaps, so as to take the enemy by surprise? Perhaps.

Most of the men were dead, she knew—but all of them? Could some have found cover? Might some be lying low, waiting for a chance?

They had no chance, not out here almost twenty kilometers from shelter in the middle of winter, obviously outgunned by an enemy they could not see. If the enemy did not kill them, the cold would.

She was still having trouble breathing, she realized; even now that she had had time to recover, she was having difficulty getting air into her lungs. Snow was blocking her nose and mouth. She was lying on one arm, while the other, the one that had been injured by the blue-white bolt, would not move; the weight of the snow held her down.

Then she heard the crunching of heavy footsteps on the slope just above her, and she stopped trying to move.

The enemy. The enemy was there, no more than a meter away, looking over his handiwork.

She held utterly still, waiting, staring out at the narrow area she could see through her one uncovered eye.

The man still lay there, and she tried to make out who it was—Mikhail Alexandrovich Barankin, was it? Yes, young Mikhail, almost certainly—a replacement, only arrived a fortnight before, the youngest boy in her command. Did he tremble at the sound of the approaching footsteps? Was he still alive, after all? She could see no mark on him, no blood anywhere.

The footsteps paused, no more than a meter or two from her head. Had she been spotted?

No, after only a second the footsteps proceeded; she watched intently, eager for a first clear look at their foe.

She didn't get one; instead her vision seemed to distort, so that the image of Barankin and the burning truck wavered. She blinked, trying to clear her eyes, and sipped at the air, trying to force her lungs to draw.

The distortion did not vanish, but it seemed to contract, to shrink into a small, defined area that moved across the snowfield toward Barankin. She still could not see an enemy, but now she thought she saw footprints appearing from nowhere, as if the distortion were somehow causing them.

That could not be so, she told herself. She was imagining things. The fight, her wound, her fall, the cold, they were all affecting her, disorienting her, and now she was seeing things that weren't there.

And then suddenly she saw something that she could not believe was a hallucination, that she could not accept as a trick of the cold or a smear on her goggles or anything but either reality or the onset of utter madness.

A creature appeared out of nowhere, a creature that stood upright like a man, but was clearly not human; arcs of electric fire crawled over its body for a moment as it appeared, and then vanished once it stood fully exposed. She could see its shape clearly in the firelight.

It was taller than a man, well over two meters in height. Its face was smooth, angular metal, and for a moment Ligacheva wondered whether the Americans had devised some sort of killer robot and sent it here for testing.

The thing did not move like a machine, though, and its body was proportioned and constructed almost like that of a living being.

Then she looked at the rest of it and saw that it was no machine; the metal face was a mask. It wore a belt and some sort of shoulder harness that held equipment; black cuffs covered its forearms.

But the rest of its body was almost bare, much of it hidden only by some sort of mesh. Its skin shone an unhealthy yellow in the firelight—and she could see plenty of skin through the mesh. She marveled at that; how could anything expose bare flesh to this burning cold?

This was obviously the creature that had left those tracks in the snow; she could not see its feet clearly, but she thought she saw not boots, but sandals, and curving black claws. That explained the claw marks—but how could it stand to expose its feet to the cold? Why wasn't it dead of frostbite?

It wasn't; she simply had to accept that.

It stood over Barankin, then suddenly stooped down. One hand gripped the boy's head—his *entire head* fit neatly in the thing's palm.

The other hand drew back. Two jagged blades slid out of the black wrist cuff and snapped into place, protruding past the creature's closed fist, both blades glittering red in the glow of the burning tractor.

Up until then Ligacheva had hoped Barankin was still alive and unhurt; now she prayed that he was already dead, that he would not feel what was happening.

The thing lifted Barankin's head, and the boy shouted, "No! No!" shattering Ligacheva's hope that he would not feel anything. Then the twin blades swept down and sliced into Barankin's back, and the shout turned into a wordless scream of agony.

It didn't last long, though; a second later the creature lifted up Barankin's head, the boy's severed spine dangling, and let the headless body fall to the ground.

A pool of blood began to spread.

Then Ligacheva fainted, and that was all she saw until strong arms pulled her half-frozen from the snow—human arms, friendly arms.

The villagers, Taro's people, had smelled the smoke from the burning truck and followed the orange glow. They saw the bodies, the blood, the tracks; pragmatically they made no attempt to follow the tracks back to the source. If something was out there that could wipe out an entire squad of the modern Russian Army, they weren't interested in pursuing it armed only with knives and a couple of rifles.

They didn't see any yellow-skinned creatures. They didn't see anything that could explain the slaughter.

They did, however, recognize some of the marks in the snow on the ridge, marks where something had fallen and been buried, and they found Ligacheva and dug her out.

She was too far gone to talk, to tell them what had happened, so they took her back to her own people at the pumping station; this all took place in what seemed like a single feverish moment as the lieutenant slipped in and out of consciousness.

She saw the familiar corridors as she was hurried inside to the infirmary. She glimpsed Galyshev's face, red with anger and fear, as he bent over her bed and tried to coax sense out of her. And then she woke up in a different bed, looking up at a different ceiling, a cleaner, whiter, more brightly lit one, but she never remembered the trip, and it wasn't until the doctor told her, hours later, that she realized she was in Moscow, that they had flown her out at fantastic expense in a special emergency flight.

The massacre on the windswept Siberian ice seemed like some hideous fever dream, but one she could not shake from her thoughts; the image of that jagged double blade biting into Barankin's back, the crunching sound as the blades cut through the boy's ribs, the sight of that creature lifting its bloody trophy high so that it gleamed in the firelight, would not go away.

When at last they put her into a clean uniform and sent her to see General Ponomarenko the vision of Mikhail Barankin hung before her, like some unholy apparition, as she answered the general's questions.

She stood at attention during questioning; in light of her condition they did allow her to hold on to a rail for support as she spoke. She thought she understood why she was not permitted to sit. When she had finished her description of the nightmare she had watched from beneath her blanket of snow, she did not stop, but went on to say, "An entire army squad has been wiped out. Someone has to answer for it. I know that. The circumstances of my promotion and transfer just make it that much easier to hold me responsible, and I accept that. You need make no pretenses."

Ponomarenko smiled humorlessly and leaned back in his chair. He took a long drag on the imported cigar he held, then took a moment to carefully knock the ash into an ashtray before he looked back at Ligacheva.

"I make no secret of it, Lieutenant," he said. "I did think your promotion was a mistake. Your actions in the field, and the results, only confirm my belief." He took another puff on his cigar, then leaned forward.

"You're wrong, though, about one thing," he continued. "We aren't looking for a scapegoat this time. We don't want simple retribution. We want more than that. We want to know what *really* happened, and what's out there. And whether you have told us the truth or not, Lieutenant, you know more of what happened out there than we do." He stubbed out the cigar and pointed at her. "So, my dear," he said, "we don't want your blood. It's worse than that." He smiled coldly.

"We want you to go back."

5

What in the hell?" the technician said as he looked at the computer display. He frowned. Then he glanced up at the technicians seated to either side of him. They were quietly scanning through data downloads from spy satellites much like the one he had been receiving.

No one else seemed to see anything out of the ordinary; no one else was making comments or even looking up. That meant that whatever was responsible for what he was seeing, it wasn't a whole-system, network-wide problem. Whether it was accurate data or a glitch, it was local.

He looked back at the screen, considered for a moment, and typed in a command.

He studied the result, tried another command, and another, then finally switched back to what he'd started with.

The results didn't change. The computers said that he was, indeed, seeing what he thought he was.

He stared at it for a moment longer, then pushed back his chair and picked up a phone. It buzzed once before a voice said, "Yeah?"

"General Meeters," the tech said, "I've got something on my screen down here that I think you should see."

"Talk to me," Meeters said.

"It's satellite infrared of the Yamal Peninsula in northern Siberia. The oil fields. A big hot spot. I think you should have a look."

"Why?" Meeters asked. "You think it's a well fire? We haven't heard anything."

"I don't know what it is, General, but I really think you should look at this."

Meeters frowned. "I'll be right down." He dropped the phone and rose from his desk.

He was a week behind on his paperwork, and this wasn't going to help any—if he'd known how much paperwork was involved he wouldn't have celebrated when he made brigadier six months ago. Still, he knew his people wouldn't call him down to the surveillance room if there wasn't something there worth checking out.

He slammed his office door on the way out; moving quietly on this particular corridor was not considered good form, as no one wanted to do anything the guards might consider stealthy or suspicious. Meeters strode boldly and openly down the corridor to the surveillance room, where the guards let him pass without a word.

Shearson was the technician who had made the call; Meeters had recognized the voice. He headed directly for Shearson's station, where he looked over the tech's shoulder at the readout on the screen.

"What have we got?" he asked.

Shearson glanced up, confirmed that it was indeed the general who was asking, then tapped a quick series of keys. The screen immediately displayed an outline map of the Yamal Peninsula, with the known towns and installations neatly labeled. That was all done in fine black lines superimposed on bands of vivid color.

"This is the infrared, sir," Shearson explained. He pointed to a bar scale in the corner that explained the colors—dark green, blue, indigo, and violet were areas below freezing, and most of the screen was awash in deep, dark violet. Warmer areas were chartreuse, yellow, and so on up through orange and two shades of red.

The marked villages and pumping stations were mostly little patches of chartreuse, with a few shading to yellow. None of them showed a single pixel of orange.

However, centered on the screen, in empty wilderness a few kilometers from a greenish dot marked ASSYMA PS #12, was a fiery red spot.

"So what the hell is that?" Meeters demanded. "Is there visual?"

Shearson shook his head. "It's night there," he said, "and there's heavy cloud cover. Probably snowing."

"Anything putting out that much heat should be bright enough to see at night," Meeters pointed out. "How long has it been there? Was it there before the clouds moved in?"

Shearson shook his head again. "We don't know, sir. With the budget cuts and the lowered priority for that area, and with RIS-34 off-line right now, we've only been going over the feed for that area twice a week. Wasn't a damn thing there except ice three days ago."

"Gotta be a well fire, then," Meeters said, straightening up.

"*No*, sir," Shearson said. "I don't think so. We have visual from last week—take a look."

He tapped keys, and a new image, composed of gray shapes, superimposed itself on the existing one. Shearson pointed to the location of the red dot.

"It's at least a couple of kilometers from the pipeline and twenty or more from the nearest well-head. The Russians didn't sink any new wells in less than a week in the middle of an arctic winter, General." He tapped more keys and added, "And besides, look at this."

The grayish lines and blobs of the satellite photography vanished, then the bright colors of the infrared scan. Then a new scan appeared over the same outline map.

Again, a single bright red dot gleamed on a field of greens and blues, in that same location.

"What the hell is this one?" Meeters asked.

"Radioactivity," Shearson said. "Whatever we're looking at is hot in more ways than one. I haven't seen a mix like this since Chernobyl—though this one's different, the radiation's dropped off quickly and the heat hasn't . . ."

"*Radioactivity?*"

"Yes, sir."

"Son of a *bitch*," Meeters said. He straightened up again, turned, and shouted at the guard, "Sergeant, I want this room secured, nobody in or out without emergency authorization." Then he turned back to Shearson. "I want hard copy of all this on my desk in five minutes, and I want this wired to the White House and NORAD. Flag any intelligence reports on anything in the area—military, political, anything."

"General . . . ?" Shearson asked, startled. "What's going on? Who is it?"

"I don't know who it is," Meeters said, "or what they think they're doing—might be some kind of Soviet leftovers, might be terrorists, might be Russian nationalists gone overboard, but it's *somebody* out there."

"But whatever it is, why . . . ?" Shearson groped unsuccessfully for words.

Meeters looked at the tech in exasperation. "Think, Shearson—don't you see what that is? I mean, what the hell else could it be? You said yourself you hadn't seen anything like it since Chernobyl, and nobody builds power reactors in the middle of an oil field. Heat and radiation means that someone just cracked open a nuke—and out there in the middle of nowhere that means a *bomb*, Shearson." He jabbed a finger at the computer screen. "Someone's hauling nuclear weapons around the arctic, and it's nothing the Russians have told us about. Sure, we know they've got stuff they don't tell us, selling goodies to the Third World, and we don't like it but we live with it—but you don't smuggle nukes from Russia to Iran or Pakistan across the fucking polar ice cap. Think a minute, Shearson—what's straight across the ice cap from Siberia?"

"North America," Shearson said. "But . . ."

"Damn right," Meeters said, cutting him off. "*We* are! Maybe they've got missiles hidden out there, or maybe some damn fool's hauling them over the pole by dogsled, I don't know, but I do know that I, for one, don't want any nukes coming into my neighborhood unannounced."

"But, General, that's crazy," Shearson protested. "We aren't giving the Russians a hard time. Why would anyone try to attack us *now*?"

"Why not?" Meeters said as he headed for the door. "You got a better explanation? Since when did being crazy mean it's not happening?" He charged out of the room.

Shearson stared after him for a moment, then turned back to his console and began typing commands.

His hands shook as he typed.

General Emory Mavis, U.S. Army, frowned as he looked at the report Meeters had sent over.

Meeters thought it was a bunch of Russian crazies smuggling nukes over the pole; he didn't see that any other explanation of the data was possible. Once upon a time Mavis might have thought so, too.

Now, though, Mavis took a broader view. He had learned that a whole slew of supposedly impossible things were possible after all. Unlikely, maybe, but possible.

That understanding was what had landed him his current position, one that existed off the books; officially he was retired. Unofficially he was, all by himself, a black-budget item, listed in what few records existed as "Esoteric Threat Assessment Capability." Part of his job was to look at unlikely things and figure out just which unlikely possibility was fact. That was his specialty; that was why the

White House kept him on call. That was why they'd called him off the golf course to look at this stuff.

Another part of his job was to advise the president on just what the hell to *do* about the esoteric threats that Mavis assessed, and if necessary to take charge and see that it got done.

Meeters thought it was a bunch of crazies smuggling nukes, but that was unlikely enough that the boys in the White House basement had gotten Mavis off the best run at the back nine he'd ever had at the Burning Tree Country Club to take a look at the report, apply his expertise, and come up with something to tell the president.

Heat and radiation in the middle of the Siberian wilderness—yes, Russian warheads were the obvious explanation, but were they the *right* one?

He reached for the phone on his desk, lifted the receiver, and tapped in a number.

When he heard someone pick up on the other end, before the other could start to speak, Mavis barked, "Mavis here. Get me Charles Westfield."

He didn't bother listening to the reply; he waited until he heard Westfield's familiar voice say "Hello?"

"Dr. Westfield," Mavis said. "I need to know what sort of heat and radiation you'd see if one of the Russians' largest warheads cracked open. Fax me the figures ASAP."

"Tonight?" Westfield said, startled.

"*Now,*" Mavis told him. "As soon as we're done talking. You have the number?"

"I'm not sure . . ."

"Got a pen?"

Ten minutes later the fax machine whirred and began extruding paper.

Mavis looked at the numbers. He wasn't a physicist himself, but he'd worked with enough of this sort of material to be able to make sense of what he saw.

It didn't match what the satellites showed for Assyma. It wasn't even close.

Mavis had expected that. Five minutes later he had Westfield on the phone again.

"You're sure of these figures?" he asked.

"Yes," Westfield said. No hesitation, no qualifications—just "yes."

"Suppose a Russian nuke were damaged, enough to trigger a meltdown . . ."

"Warheads don't melt down," Westfield interrupted. "You've got several times critical mass of highly enriched metal there—you put it together and it's going to explode, not just melt into slag."

"All right, it's not a warhead, then," Mavis said. "Let me fax you something, and you tell me what you make of it." He pulled out the printout of the raw satellite data, before Shearson or Meeters had added any comments or interpretation, and fed it into the fax.

"It's not a warhead, damaged or otherwise," Westfield told him. "And it's not a meltdown—too much heat, not enough neutron emission for a meltdown. Might be a low-yield burst of some kind—are there any seismic reports?"

"Good question," Mavis replied.

It took hours and dozens of calls—to seismologists, CIA analysts, and several agencies that weren't supposed to exist—before General Mavis was satisfied.

Whatever was out there in Siberia had appeared with a shock wave that fit the profile of a fair-sized meteorite impact rather than any sort of explosion—but if something big had fallen from the sky, there was no trace of its descent. It hadn't shown up on the tracking radar that constantly scanned the skies all over Earth. The impact profile, working from seismographic records, indicated that the object had been traveling southeast at a fairly shallow angle when it hit; if it had been a meteor, then it should have been spotted on several radar screens.

The heat of impact should have dissipated fairly quickly, but that wasn't what the infrared showed. The radiation profile didn't fit a meteor, either.

The CIA didn't have much to tell him about human activity; the technical stuff was comparatively easy to get and safe to pass along, while ground-level reports were risky. However, they said that a low-ranking officer had been rushed from Assyma to Moscow just hours ago, and was debriefed by several generals. Something was going on out there, all right—but the CIA didn't know what it was. They didn't think the Russians knew exactly what was happening, either.

Mavis nodded as he considered that.

It all fit.

Something hot had fallen from the sky, something that hadn't shown on radar, something that didn't act like any sort of natural object, something that the Russians seemed as puzzled by as anyone . . .

A spaceship, Mavis thought.

He had dealt with spaceships before. It was something everyone kept quiet about, for several reasons, but Mavis knew about some previous visits by spaceships. None had been quite like this, though. Some parts of the profile matched, others didn't.

Assuming that this time the ship hadn't landed under its own power explained the mismatches perfectly.

All the other visitors had been the same species; Mavis wondered, as he looked over his own scribbled notes, whether perhaps Earth was their private preserve. Maybe there were cosmic NO TRESPASSING signs out there that kept away everyone else.

Whether there were signs or not, Mavis guessed that these were probably the same fellows, back again. And if that was the case, then Mavis knew who to call in to deal with them.

He reached for the phone.

6

General Philips sat at his desk and stared at the empty shot glass, rolling it back and forth in his hands, trying to decide whether to refill it.

There was a time when he would have sworn he would never drink on duty. He snorted quietly. He'd been a naive little punk back then.

And after all, was he *really* on duty? Oh, sure, they said he was. They said he was on call. They gave him this little space here, his own little cubbyhole of an office, with nothing in it but a desk and a phone and the shot glass and a bottle of bourbon, and said he was on call, that he'd be getting new orders any day.

They had lied to him, of course. He wasn't on duty here; he was just out of the way. And nobody ever said a man shouldn't drink when he'd been shoved aside because his superiors thought he'd screwed up.

And Philips didn't doubt that his superiors thought he'd screwed up big time six months ago, when big-game hunters from outer space had been using New York City as their private preserve.

The brass had known for years that the aliens existed. They'd known that the monsters had been hunting humans in tropical jungles for decades, and they'd kept it all quiet—but you can't keep it all quiet when people start getting butchered in the middle of an American city!

They'd done a damn good job covering it up; Philips had started it himself, before his "transfer." Still, there were rumors, there were people who'd seen too much, and Philips was pretty sure that his superiors thought that those rumors and witnesses were his fault.

His superiors hadn't been there, damn it. They hadn't been there on the streets, watching a bunch of alien monsters shooting it out with cops and hoodlums. They'd been willing to write off a couple of dozen civilians gone for trophies if it meant avoiding trouble with the aliens, but they hadn't *been* there, watching it happen, seeing innocent people slaughtered.

Philips had been there, and at the end he'd come in on the human side, fighting the monsters, in defiance of his orders. He'd *had* to.

But it hadn't made any difference—the creatures had left because they got bored and the weather turned cool, not because they'd lost or gotten angry.

The big brass didn't believe that. They thought Philips and those two cops, Schaefer and Rasche, had chased the aliens away. They'd wanted a piece of the aliens' gadgetry to play with, and they thought Philips had screwed up in not getting them something.

But they hadn't seen how careful those damned extraterrestrials were about making sure their precious technology didn't fall into the hands of the people they preyed upon. There hadn't been a *chance* to capture anything.

The brass didn't know what it had been like. He hadn't screwed up, damn it—he'd been handed a disaster, and he'd done everything he could to keep it from getting any worse than it already was. No one could have done better without just shooting Schaefer and Rasche—and no one could have known to do that until it was too late.

Of course, his superiors had never *told* him to his face that he'd screwed up—they'd probably been afraid that he'd go to the press if they booted him out or dressed him down. No, they'd just waited a couple of weeks, transferred him, given him this office, and told him to wait here until they called with his new orders.

He'd asked about the programs he'd started, whether he'd still be training Captain Lynch's team, whether Smithers and the rest of the New York office would still be tracking down possible incidents, whether the Pentagon team would continue checking incoming electronic intelligence for signs of the aliens, and they'd said not to worry about any of that; it would all be taken care of. He was just to wait until they called.

That was almost six months ago, and the phone hadn't rung yet.

He'd finished up all his paperwork the first

month. Then he'd started bringing books he'd always wanted to read. Around the third month he started bringing a bottle of bourbon along with the books.

By the fifth month he was just bringing the bourbon. Another couple of weeks and he doubted he'd bother coming in at all. It had taken a while, but he'd gotten the hint. That phone was never going to ring. Lynch was probably training antiterrorist teams somewhere, and Smithers was probably training terrorists for the CIA. The whole thing was over.

He couldn't go to the press now. The news wasn't hot. The people in charge had had all the time they needed to cover everything up, to get all the stories to match, all the messes cleaned up, and all the evidence neatly tucked out of sight.

He could argue with them, of course. He could complain, he could demand something to do, he could go all the way to the president if he had to.

There wasn't any point in it, though. If he made a stink, they might give him something to do, or they might just retire him, but one thing seemed pretty sure—they weren't going to put him back on the assignment he'd had before, the one he really wanted, dealing with those things, those killers, those monsters from outer space.

That was what he really cared about. There was so much potential there. The technology to travel between stars, all those incredible weapons the things had, their invisibility screens—if the right people had all that, it would mean a whole new world, a whole new *universe*. If one of the starships those things used could be captured and reverse-engineered, the Apollo flights to the moon would look like a soapbox derby by comparison—people would go to the *stars*. Entire worlds might well be out there for the taking—resources and wealth beyond imagining! If there were other alien civilizations besides the hunters somewhere out there in the galaxy, friendlier ones, then humanity wouldn't be alone anymore. That would change *everything*.

Even if that wasn't possible, even if human beings didn't get a stardrive out of it, at the very least those things had weapons and technologies that could put the U.S. so far ahead of the rest of the world that dealing with bozos like Saddam Hussein or Muammar Qaddafi would be no more trouble than swatting a few flies.

This was the biggest thing anyone had *ever* been involved in—it had been his own private playground, and they had taken it away from him.

He hoped they hadn't just abandoned everything. Maybe they had put someone else on it, someone they trusted more. Maybe someone like Lynch was in charge.

He hoped so.

Maybe, he told himself, it wasn't as bleak as he thought. Maybe they really did intend to call him, and those things just hadn't been back to Earth since the New York affair, so there hadn't been any need for him. Maybe they'd get around to calling him eventually.

Or maybe the big brass honestly thought those things were gone for good.

Hell, maybe they *were* gone for good—that whole mess must've been embarrassing for them, too. They'd come to Earth looking for a good time, or maybe to avenge the hunter Dutch had killed all those years ago, and they'd wound up getting two or three of their boys notched; if they were an outfit running the equivalent of paid safaris, that wouldn't have looked good in the ads back home. Or if they had some sort of noninterference rules, they'd blown those out of the water when they landed their ship in the middle of Third Avenue.

Hushing all that up must've been a bitch, Philips thought. Even on a Sunday morning, there must have been a hundred witnesses.

Maybe the top brass thought that the trouble had all happened because people had tried to interfere. Maybe they thought there was no way to get that technology, so they just wanted to ignore the aliens now. Even when Philips had been running the show he'd usually had orders to let the hunters have their fun, kill a few people, take a few trophies—don't make 'em mad. The brass had always been more worried than eager, more concerned that they not get the aliens mad enough to start an actual war than with having anyone learn anything from the spacefaring bastards.

And now they weren't giving Philips a *chance* to interfere and maybe piss the creatures off. The big brass was keeping him waiting here, at an empty desk, staring at a phone that never rang . . .

The phone rang.

At first Philips didn't even notice. He heard the sound, but it didn't register. He didn't recognize it as anything that concerned him; it was just more of the background noise that was always present.

Then it rang again, and that time it penetrated. He jerked as if he'd been shot, dropped the empty glass, and snatched up the receiver.

"Philips here," he barked into the receiver.

He was trembling.

7

Rasche awoke slowly, his mind hazy; he didn't really remember where he was.

He lived in Bluecreek, Oregon, he remembered that much—he and his wife, Shari, and their two boys. They'd moved out here to be safe, after that mess in New York.

He wasn't at home now, though, was he? Whatever he was lying on, it didn't feel like an ordinary bed. He opened his eyes.

At first he saw only darkness. Then bright light, painfully bright, cut through the dark, blinding him. He closed his eyes again, still trying to collect his thoughts.

That mess back in New York . . . who were those things, really? What were they? Why were they there? Would they come back?

Would they come back for *him*?

Schaefer had had them all figured out, but

54

Rasche had never really understood it. Hunters from space, yeah—but why? How did they decide who to hunt? Where would he be safe—anywhere? Was Bluecreek far enough away?

He couldn't stop thinking about them, couldn't stop remembering the strange masks and the hideous faces underneath, their yellow flesh and black talons, the dripping blood and mutilated bodies of their victims.

He blinked. He felt as if he had been drugged—had he? He couldn't remember. He still couldn't remember where he was, how he had gotten there. He tried to see through the light, through the mental haze.

A mask—he saw a mask hovering over him. And long yellow fingers were reaching toward his face.

It was one of *them,* he realized—one of those things from outer space!

"He's awake . . ." someone said.

Rasche forced himself to act, suddenly and decisively. He wasn't a young man, he looked overweight and out of shape, but he could still move fast and hard when he needed to, and he moved now, lunging at the thing in the mask, his hands reaching for its throat as he shouted, "Not again! You won't get away again! This time I'm taking you down with me!"

His foe went over backward and tumbled to the floor. Rasche landed on his opponent's chest, and that unbearably bright light was behind him instead of in his eyes, so that he could see clearly again.

A woman shrieked, "Sheriff Rasche, please! Stop it!"

Rasche looked down and saw that the shadowy figure wasn't what he had thought. The mask was white paper over gauze, not alien metal; the throat in his hands was human. The yellow fingers were rubber gloves. And Rasche knew he couldn't have knocked over one of those alien predators anywhere near so easily. He released his hold.

Then at last the mental haze cleared, and Rasche realized he was kneeling atop his dentist.

"Dr. Krelmore," he said, suddenly remembering the man's name.

Krelmore made a choking noise.

"I'm sorry," Rasche said as he got off his victim. "The gas . . . I mean . . ."

"The *gas*?" Krelmore said as his hygienist helped him up off the floor.

"I was imagining things that weren't there," Rasche said. "Hallucinating, I guess."

"Hallucinating?" Krelmore brushed himself off. "I'm just a dentist, Sheriff, but I never saw anyone react like that just to the gas." He coughed. "Your filling's all done, but maybe . . . maybe you'd be better off consulting, you know, a psychiatrist or something."

Rasche shook his head. "I've seen enough psychiatrists to diagnose the entire state of Florida," he said. More to himself than the others, he added, "Jesus, I really thought I was *over* it." He looked at Dr. Krelmore. "I had this real bad time . . ." he began.

Then he caught himself. Telling his dentist that he'd been involved in a secret war against alien monsters on the streets of New York was not exactly a good career move.

"Look, Doc," he said, "I'm really sorry for what happened. I . . . I'd appreciate it if you could keep this under your hat." He managed a sickly smile.

"I've been under a lot of stress lately, y'know? New place, new job, I'm still getting settled in."

"Sure," Krelmore said, rubbing his neck—the red marks left by Rasche's chokehold were already fading. "Sure, no problem, Sheriff. Your secret's safe with me." He forced a weak grin in response to Rasche's smile. "Every time they show *Marathon Man* on TV, it's the same damn thing. You'd think I'd be used to it by now."

"Nobody's ever . . ." the hygienist began, then stopped as both men turned unhappily to face her, afraid she was going to say something they'd all regret.

"Well, we've had some upset patients before," she said, "but I think you're the first one to actually take Dr. Krelmore down like that."

Krelmore's smile reappeared. "Best two falls out of three?" he asked.

No one quite managed to laugh.

Ten minutes later Rasche was out on the streets of Bluecreek, thinking hard as he automatically scanned his surroundings, cop fashion.

He didn't like losing control like that. Yeah, he'd been out of it from the gas, but trying to strangle a harmless tooth doctor was not a good sign, even so. He'd been the local sheriff in Bluecreek for a little over four months now, and he'd mostly thought he'd been settling in nicely. He'd thought that he'd left all the freaks and crazies behind when he quit the NYPD and went west, but now he wondered whether maybe one of the craziest hadn't moved out west right along with him, right inside his own head.

He walked on automatically as he thought, taking in everything around him, unconsciously classifying everyone he saw into one of three categories, the traditional New York cop triage. The three categories were cops, citizens, and scum; back in the Big Apple he'd always seen a mix, but here in Bluecreek he only seemed to see citizens.

That had been the whole point of moving here, of course, but it still didn't seem entirely natural. He'd spent almost his whole life in New York; if it hadn't been for those monsters from Planet X, he'd undoubtedly still be there, probably still working homicide or narco with his partner Schaefer, finishing out his time until retirement.

The spaceships and the all-out firefight on Third Avenue had been too much for him, though. He'd left. He'd found the job as sheriff, gathered up Shari and the kids, and come out here where it was safe.

Or safer, anyway. He glanced at the sky. He couldn't be sure *anywhere* was really safe, but Bluecreek seemed like a pretty good bet. Rasche had been pleased to get the job offer. He'd sent out his résumé from the hospital, and the reply from Bluecreek had been waiting when he was released. He'd grabbed it.

He'd asked Schaef to come with him, but the big man had refused. Rasche had even offered him a job as deputy, and Schaefer had smiled so broadly Rasche thought he might actually laugh—which would have been a first, Schaefer actually laughing at anything Rasche said.

Rasche had to admit that the idea of Schaefer playing Barney Fife to Rasche's Sheriff Taylor was pretty absurd, but he'd kept asking as long as he could.

It hadn't worked. Schaefer had stayed in New York.

It wasn't that Schaefer loved the city all that much; he didn't. Sometimes Rasche thought Schaefer hated the place. And it wasn't that he'd never lived anywhere else; Schaefer wasn't a native New Yorker. Rasche thought he'd grown up in Pennsylvania somewhere, though he wasn't sure—Schaefer had never really said where he came from.

No, Schaefer stayed in New York because he wasn't going to let those alien things drive him out, and he wasn't going to let the government order him around. Rasche knew that and understood it—other people had wanted Schaefer to go away, people Schaefer didn't like, and that was the surest way there was to get Schaef to stay put. As long as the feds wanted Schaefer out of New York, he wasn't going to leave the city—not for Rasche, not for anyone.

Besides, Rasche thought, Schaefer was still pissed off about the government covering up the mess, still pissed off that they hadn't told him what had happened to his brother Dutch, the covert operative, after Dutch had disappeared on a rescue mission in Central America. Staying in New York meant that Schaefer would have more people to take that anger out on.

Rasche unlocked the front door of the split level that still didn't quite feel like home, the split level that was about three times the size of their old place in Queens, and stepped inside. As he did, a photo of Schaefer and himself, standing on an end table in the living room, caught his eye; he ambled over and picked it up.

That was right after they'd taken down a vicious little bastard who had called himself Errol G. Rasche remembered it well as he looked down at his own face. There he was, a big grin making his mustache bristle while Schaefer's face could have been carved out of stone.

He wondered what Schaefer was doing right at that moment. He wondered whether Schaefer still had nightmares about those creatures.

He wondered whether Schaefer ever had nightmares about *anything*. Schaefer didn't seem the nightmare-having type, somehow.

Nightmare-*causing*, yeah; Rasche could think of a few people who might have nightmares about Schaefer. He smiled at the thought.

He'd have to call Schaef, just to chat, sometime soon.

The smile vanished. He needed to talk to *somebody* about those things, somebody other than the psychologists who thought the aliens were stress-induced hallucinations, somebody other than Shari, who, sweet as she was, never knew what to say about the grimmer aspects of Rasche's work.

Yeah, he'd call Schaefer soon.

Very soon.

8

Detective Schaefer stepped into his own office and stopped dead, staring at the man seated behind the desk.

The stranger, caught off guard, stared back, frozen there with one hand reaching out for a framed photograph. His expression was smothered surprise.

He was a man in a conservative and expensive suit, with a conservative and expensive haircut, a man who looked as if he'd be more at home on Wall Street than Police Plaza. Right now, though, he was at 1 Police Plaza, in the headquarters of the New York Police Department, sitting in Schaefer's chair, holding a photo of Schaefer and Rasche that was the only ornament on Schaefer's desk, and staring at Schaefer.

After a moment of utter silence, Schaefer said, "Go ahead, make yourself at home. Take a look around. Maybe you'll find some quarters under the seat cushion."

"Ah," the stranger said, carefully putting down the photo he'd been looking at. "My name is Smithers, Detective Schaefer." He rose, holding out a hand to shake as he came around the desk. "I've been sent . . ."

Schaefer ignored the hand. He had recognized something about the other's attitude. "You're one of those army goons," he interrupted. "Like Philips and the others. The ones who thought they could handle our friends on Third Avenue last summer."

"I, ah . . ." Smithers began, quickly lowering the proffered hand.

He didn't deny the connection, which was all the confirmation Schaefer needed. Schaefer cut him off. "I've got work to do, Smithers," he said. "*Real* work. Whatever it is you came to say, spit it out. Then leave." He pulled off his jacket.

"Yes, I . . ." Smithers said. Then he saw Schaefer's face and cut to the chase. "There's been an incident, Detective Schaefer. An entirely new occurrence. We believe your expertise, due to your previous experience in related matters, could prove invaluable should the event develop beyond current expectations . . ."

"Jesus, do you people spend your lunch hours memorizing a goddamn thesaurus?" Schaefer demanded as he turned and opened his locker. "Let me guess what you're actually telling me, shall I? The boys are back in town and you'd like me to check it out, for old times' sake."

"Exactly," Smithers said. "There are some new elements, however . . ."

"Fuck new elements," Schaefer said as he hung

up his jacket and slipped off his shoulder holster. "I've got a job to do here."

"Of course, we would clear your status with your chief and any other applicable agencies . . ."

"I'll bet you would." Schaefer unbuttoned his shirt, speaking as he did. "You don't seem to get it, Smithers, so let me spell it out. The Schaefer boys have put in their time as far as Philips and the rest of you are concerned. If you and the rest of your gang of hotshot special agents, or whatever you call yourselves, want to go for another tag-team match with those ugly mothers from outer space, you go right ahead, have at it." He pulled off the shirt and slid it onto a hanger, exposing a body that would have done Arnold Schwarzenegger proud. "But you can leave me right out of it."

"But, Detective . . ." Smithers began.

Schaefer taped a wire to his chest, holding a tiny microphone in place. "No," he said.

"I'm sure that if . . ."

Schaefer continued to install the surveillance equipment as he said, "What part of 'no' didn't you understand?"

"Damn it, Detective, will you let me finish a sentence?" Smithers shouted.

"Why should I?" Schaefer asked. "Besides, I just did." With the wires securely in place, he reached in the locker and pulled out a gaudy pink-and-green shirt, the sort of thing the tackier pimps on Seventh Avenue wore.

Smithers fumed for a moment, then said, "I'd think you'd *want* a chance to get involved in this."

Schaefer started buttoning the shirt, then looked at Smithers. "Why? Are they in New York again?"

"Well, no," Smithers admitted.

"I knew it," Schaefer said, looking back down at the buttons. "I'd have *smelled* them if they were here." He finished buttoning the shirt, pulled a brown leather coat out of the locker, then turned to Smithers and said, "Listen up, army boy. If they aren't in New York, I'm not interested. I don't like those sons of bitches, but there are a lot of people in this world I don't like, including you." He tugged on one sleeve. "I've done my time, Smithers. So did my brother. He lost his entire squad to them; I got my city shot up and lost my partner. We took down a few of those ugly bastards along the way, we did our best, and I'm willing to call it even if they stay off my turf. You tell me they're not on my turf, so you can just go to hell, and take General Philips with you." He pulled on the other sleeve.

"Your 'turf' is just New York?"

"Damn right." He straightened the coat. "I may think I'm pretty hot shit, but I'm not up to playing cop for the whole goddamned world. New York's big enough for anyone."

"So you won't consider helping us?"

"I told you 'no' once already."

"That's your final word?"

"My *real* 'final word' would probably get me arrested," Schaefer said, giving Smithers a shove toward the door. "Now get out of my office before I sprinkle you with salt and watch you melt on the sidewalk like the slug you are." He pushed Smithers out and closed the door.

That done, he glanced at the clock. Despite that little chat he still had a few minutes to spare before he had to be in position.

He looked at the closed door. The man in the

suit was making no effort to get back in, which was good—but that didn't mean it was the end of the matter.

Even if Philips and his buddies were willing to let it drop, that didn't mean Schaefer was. He'd been looking for Philips in his spare time for months, and hadn't found him—but now he might have a fresh lead.

"Smithers, huh?" he muttered to himself. "If that's a real name, I just might want to look him up later. We might have a nice little chat about Dutch." He fished a scrap of paper from the pile on his desk, found a pen, and scribbled a quick note to himself—just two names, "Smithers" and "Philips," with an arrow connecting them.

Schaefer's brother Dutch had disappeared years ago while working for Philips. Schaefer was certain that Dutch had run up against one of those alien big-game hunters, down there in Central America where Philips and his boys had been playing around in the local politics. Dutch and his boys had walked right into its hunting ground, and the thing had butchered Dutch's entire team—but Dutch had apparently killed it and gotten out alive.

And *then* he'd vanished, and Schaefer was pretty damn sure that Philips knew more about that disappearance than he'd admitted.

And after last summer's debacle Philips had disappeared, too—into the Pentagon somewhere, probably. Schaefer had resented that; he had wanted to have a friendly little talk with Philips.

This Smithers might be able to lead him to Philips, and maybe they could make some kind of a deal. He might just help Philips out after all, if the two of them could agree on a few details. He didn't like those big ugly bastards from outer space, and despite what he'd told Smithers, a rematch wasn't completely out of the question.

Any deal they might make would have to be on Schaefer's terms, though. He wasn't going to come running whenever Philips called. And sending Smithers here to fetch him had just pissed him off.

Schaefer would deal with Smithers and his boss when and where he chose—which wasn't here or now. For one thing, he wasn't going to tackle any sort of serious negotiating here at Police Plaza, with a couple of hundred cops around who might have their own ideas about what was appropriate bargaining behavior. No, they'd meet somewhere private, at a time and place of Schaefer's choosing, when he was good and ready, and when that happened the agenda was going to start with Dutch, not with those alien freaks.

And it wouldn't be any time all that soon, because Schaefer had a bust to attend to, one that he and his men had been setting up for weeks. Once that was out of the way, *then* he'd have time to worry about Dutch, General Philips, and a bunch of bloodthirsty goons from space.

He dropped the note on the desk and left.

9

Schaefer turned and looked out through the storefront, trying to appear casual—or as casual as he ever did, at any rate.

He was standing in a small shop in the Village, a place called Collectors World that sold comic books, baseball cards, and other such things, all of it over-priced kid stuff, in Schaefer's opinion. He was pretending to talk to the shop's manager, a balding guy named Jon Cohen, but he was actually looking out the front window at the man in the driver's seat of a brown van that had just parked illegally at the opposite sidewalk.

The van was late; Schaefer had been in here killing time for a good three minutes, waiting for it.

"Testing, one two three, testing, one two three," he said in a conversational tone. "This wire better be working, Rawlings, because I'm going in in about two minutes, before these clowns talk me into buying any funny books."

The driver held up a hand, displaying thumb and forefinger in a circle—the "okay" sign. The mike was live.

"Okay, boys," Schaefer said as he strode toward the door, pushing past a clerk who'd also given his name as John, "we're on. Remember, nobody moves in until Baby coughs up the dope. I want her for dealing, not just for some candy-ass zoning violation."

He marched out onto the sidewalk and across the street, headed for a kitchenware shop—a shop that, according to the dealers in the vicinity and NYPD's own undercover operatives, happened to be the local headquarters for wholesale cocaine. A cold winter wind ripped down the street, flapping his leather coat, but Schaefer ignored it.

In the back of the brown van one of the three cops manning the monitoring equipment muttered, "Thank God Schaefer's here to tell us our jobs, hey? For a second there I was almost feeling competent."

His companions grinned nervously.

"Shut up," Rawlings said from the driver's seat. "You guys be ready."

A bell jingled as Schaefer stepped into the kitchenware shop. He looked around at the cluttered shelves and empty aisles; the only other person in the place was the woman behind the counter, who seemed out of place amid saucepans and spatulas. She wore fishnet stockings, an elaborately teased blond wig, and makeup as thick as Tammy Faye Bakker's, and looked as much at home among kitchenware as a coyote among kittens.

Schaefer knew her as Baby. *Everyone* in this neighborhood knew her as Baby.

"Glad you could make it, big man," she said. "Could I interest you in some Fiestaware?"

Schaefer grinned. "No way," he replied, doing his best impression of a happy-go-lucky kid. "Coke sticks to the Teflon when you cook it down."

The woman smiled back. "No problem. I'll toss in a couple of cans of Pam."

In the truck one of the cops muttered, "Asshole. Coke doesn't stick to Teflon."

"C'mon, Schaef," Rawlings said, knowing Schaefer couldn't hear him. "Don't swap dumb jokes with the broad, just make the damn buy!"

In the back, one of the techs glanced up from the equipment, then nudged his neighbor and pointed out the back window. "Oh, great," he said. "We've got company."

A man in a ragged trench coat was approaching the van unsteadily, standing on tiptoe as if trying to peer in through the windows in the rear doors. The windows were covered with one-way foil, so he wouldn't see anything, but still, no one involved with the operation wanted anything to draw any attention to the van.

"Some homeless geek looking for a smash and grab," the cop nearest the door said. "Want me to get out there and shoo him away?"

Rawlings shook his head. "Not when we're in Baby's line of sight," he said. "Just keep an eye on him."

"Got it," the man by the rear door said. He turned to look out the back window again just in time to see the derelict pull a .357 from under his trench coat.

"Oh, my God . . ." the cop said, just before the bum pulled the trigger and the plastic window shattered. Half a second later, before anyone could react, a second shot took the top off the cop's head.

The third shot punched through another cop's throat; the fourth missed, and Rawlings actually got off a shot of his own before a slug went through his right eye.

Rawlings's shot missed the "derelict" completely and ricocheted off the second story of an office building half a block away.

The last cop, a technician who'd never fired his gun outside the department shooting range before, was still fumbling with the flap on his holster when the "derelict's" sixth bullet took him down.

"What the hell?" Schaefer said, whirling at the sound of gunfire.

Something had gone wrong; he knew that much instantly. He didn't know yet what had gone wrong, but it had to be bad. He'd heard six shots, one after another, from a high-caliber handgun—*not* anything his backup was carrying. For a moment he completely forgot about the woman he'd been trying to bust.

That was a mistake.

"You should have gone for the pans, sweetheart," Baby said, pulling a .45 from under the counter. As she did, a big man with a shaved head, tattoos, and a pump-action shotgun stepped out of the back room. The shotgun was aimed directly at Schaefer's head.

"Don't you think so, Detective Schaefer?" Baby said. "If you'd just come in for a nice set of aluminumware we might've avoided a whole shitload of trouble."

Schaefer stared at Baby for a moment, considering the automatic in her hand, then turned and looked over the punk with the shotgun.

The gun was held nice and steady, not wavering at all, and Schaefer could see that finger crooked on the trigger, ready to pull. Baby's hand was steady, too.

Reluctantly Schaefer raised his hands. He might have tried jumping one opponent, but the combination of the two was too much.

He wanted to know what the hell had just happened outside, where his backup was, whether he still *had* any backup, but it didn't look as if anyone was going to answer his questions just now. He had a sneaking suspicion that if he headed for the door, he'd catch a bullet in the back.

Baby strolled around the counter, showing off those fishnets and her bloodred spike heels. She stepped up to Schaefer and shoved the .45 under his chin. "When are you cops going to *learn*?" she said. "Nothing goes down around here that Baby doesn't know about." She reached out and ran the fingers of her left hand under the leather coat and across Schaefer's shirt while her right held the gun in place. The gesture was a mockery of eroticism; Schaefer knew she wasn't fondling him. She was looking for something.

She found it. Her fingertips brushed the wire under Schaefer's shirt, and she ripped the shirt open, exposing the tiny microphone.

"Cute little thing," she said.

"You like it?" Schaefer said. "Keep going—you might find a CD player strapped to—"

"Shut up!" she said, slapping the .45 across his face. It stung, but Schaefer didn't feel anything broken or bleeding—Baby had just been making a point. If she wanted to, he didn't doubt she could do far worse, so he knew she hadn't been trying to hurt him.

Not yet, anyway.

Just then, before Schaefer could reply or Baby could comment further, the ripping sound of nearby full-auto gunfire interrupted the conversation.

The three in the shop froze.

"What the fuck . . ." the man with the shotgun said—the first words Schaefer had heard him speak. He had a squeaky tenor that didn't match his broad shoulders. He kept the shotgun trained on Schaefer, glancing uneasily back and forth, as he headed for the shop's display window.

He didn't reach it; instead, the window reached him, bursting in a shower of shattered glass as the old man in the trench coat came flying through it amid another burst of machine-gun fire.

"Son of a *bitch*!" Baby said. She turned and ran for the back door, the .45 still in her hand.

Schaefer didn't worry about that; he'd stationed a man out back, just in case, and if that cop couldn't handle Baby, then the department was in worse shape than Schaefer thought.

The shotgunner, unaware of his boss's sudden exit, picked himself up from the welter of broken glass and pumped two rounds into the street at random.

"Fuck!" he screamed. "Baby, it's fucked somehow! They got Arturo!"

"What do you know, Einstein," Schaefer said. "So they did!" He had no weapon, since he'd thought they might check him out before closing the buy, and the other man still had the shotgun, but Schaefer didn't hesitate before launching himself in a flying tackle.

The two men landed in a clatter of kitchenware; the shotgun put another round through the shop ceiling before flying from its owner's hands.

The man turned over in Schaefer's grip, though, and locked his hands around the detective's throat.

"Die, motherfucker!" he said. He squeezed.

Those shoulders weren't just for looks, Schaefer realized. "Potty-mouth," he grunted, forcing the words out in a harsh whisper. "And speaking of pots . . ." He picked up a heavy-duty frying pan from the store's scattered stock and slammed it down on his opponent's head.

The grip on his neck suddenly loosened.

"Take a look," Schaefer said as he pulled free. He held up the pan. "Drugs," he said. Then he slammed it down on the other man's head again, just to be sure. "That's drugs on your brain. Your brain on drugs. Whatever."

He climbed to his feet, tossed the pan aside, then asked his unconscious foe, "Any questions?"

"Yeah, I got a question," Baby said from the back-room doorway. "You gonna run, or you gonna die?"

She was holding an M-16, Schaefer realized. What's more, she was pointing it directly at him. She hadn't been fleeing at all when she'd left; she'd just been going back for more firepower.

He dove for cover behind a rack of flour and sugar canisters as she opened fire, and then he began crawling, looking for something he could use as shelter.

Baby continued to spray bullets into the merchandise for another few seconds, until the click of an empty chamber told her she'd used up her ammunition.

"*Damn it!*" she shouted as she realized she had missed him. She yanked the spent clip and fumbled with a new one. "Where are you, big boy? Come out, come out wherever you are!"

This would have been Schaefer's chance, while Baby was reloading, if he'd been somewhere he could have gotten at her. He wasn't. He didn't have a gun, and Baby was on the other side of two aisles of kitchen gadgets.

By the time the fresh clip was in place he had already planned his course; he slithered behind shelves full of pot holders and place mats, out of her sight, working his way behind the counter.

"Yoo hoo," Baby called. "Come on out and play, Detective Schaefer! I know you're in there."

Schaefer knew that as the echoes of gunfire and falling crockery faded and Baby's hearing recovered, she'd be able to track him by sound—there was no way he could move silently in this place, not with all the crap that had fallen off the shelves. That meant he had to move fast. He looked for a weapon.

There wasn't any. Plenty of merchants kept a gun behind the counter, the Sullivan Act notwithstanding, but all Schaefer saw under the register here were boxes of credit-card slips and the empty shelf where the .45 had been.

An idea struck him. There weren't any weapons *under* the counter . . .

He kicked the wall and said, "Damn!" Then he swung himself quickly into a squatting position, braced himself, and set the heels of his hands under the edge of the counter.

"I *heard* that, Schaefer!" Baby called. "I know where you are—now, come on out! Don't make me come in after you!"

Schaefer held his breath.

"All right, you son of a bitch, *be* like that!" she barked. "You're just making it hard on us both. Christ, a woman's work is never done." She strode over to the counter and started to lean over, finger tightening on the trigger . . .

And Schaefer straightened up from his squat, hard and fast, putting all the strength of his massive thighs into shoving the counter up into Baby's face and sending it toppling over onto her.

A moment later he stood over her, kicked the M-16 aside, then reached down and yanked the .45 from her belt. He pulled the clip, then tossed that aside as well.

He glanced around quickly. The interior of the shop was a shambles; spent cartridge casings, broken glass, and battered merchandise were scattered everywhere. Cold winter air was pouring in from the street. The dead man called Arturo was sprawled just inside the remains of the main display window; the unconscious punk Schaefer had crowned with the frying pan lay nearby.

And a dazed but still conscious Baby lay right in front of him, glaring up at him.

"You're under arrest," he said. "You have the right to remain silent . . ."

The crunch of glass alerted him; Schaefer turned to see Smithers and three other men in black suits and overcoats standing in the shattered window.

Two of them held assault rifles of a design Schaefer didn't recognize, and Schaefer suddenly

realized who'd shot out the front window—and
Arturo.

"Come on, Schaefer," Smithers said. "You're
coming with us."

"The hell I am," Schaefer replied.

"We've got our orders," Smithers said. "And all
the authorization we need. I tried asking nicely;
now I'm *telling* you. You're coming with us."

"And I'm telling you I'm not," Schaefer replied.
"I'm taking Baby and her little playmate in, and I'm
calling the meat wagon for Arturo there, and then
in a day or so, when the paperwork's all squared
away, I'm going to sweat some information out of
Baby."

Smithers signaled to the man who didn't have a
rifle; that man drew a 9mm handgun from a shoulder
holster, stepped over Arturo's corpse, then neatly,
unhesitatingly, put a bullet through Baby's head.

She hadn't had time to realize what was
coming; the expression on what was left of her face
was mere puzzlement, not fear.

"Christ!" Schaefer exclaimed, staring down at
the body in shock.

"Him, too," Smithers said with a nod, and the
shotgunner's brains were added to the mess on the
carpet.

"Smithers, you bastard!" Schaefer shouted.

"Just one less drug-dealing bitch to worry
about," Smithers said. "We've got more important
things to discuss."

"Like your funeral," Schaefer said. "You asshole, we've been tracking Baby for *months*! She
could have delivered names, dates, suppliers . . ."

"Oh, for . . ." Smithers began. Then he caught
himself. "You still don't understand, do you,

Schaefer?" he said. "We have a *problem,* a *big* problem, much bigger than any drug network. We need your help, and you're going to give it to us, no matter what."

"I understand well enough," Schaefer said coldly. "I understand that I liked Baby a whole lot more than I like *you,* Smithers."

"We're up against something a lot more important than drug dealers, Schaefer," Smithers said. "Something a lot worse." He nodded to his men. "Take him."

"*You're* worse than the dealers!" Schaefer shouted as the men with machine guns stepped up on either side and trained their weapons on Schaefer's head. Schaefer froze.

The other man holstered his 9mm, buttoned his jacket, then stepped forward, toward Schaefer, reaching in a pocket of his overcoat as he did.

"You're worse than all of them," Schaefer said as the agent pulled out a black case and snapped it open, revealing a loaded hypodermic needle. "At least the people I bust know they've done something wrong."

The man in the black coat slid the needle into Schaefer's arm and pushed down on the plunger.

"You, Smithers, and the rest of you," Schaefer said, "you just don't give a shit about right or wrong . . ."

The sedative, or whatever it was, hit fast; Schaefer stayed on his feet for several more seconds before keeling over, but was unable to get out any more words or construct a coherent thought.

Even so, he thought he heard Smithers saying, "You're right, Schaefer. We don't care about right or wrong, or any kind of philosophy. What we care about is the *country*."

He wasn't sure, though; he decided that he might have imagined it.

As he began to fall to the floor he was just conscious enough to notice that the callous bastards weren't even going to catch him.

10

Looks like he's coming around, General."

Schaefer heard the words, but it took a few seconds before he could attach any meaning to them or to the thunderous beating sound that almost drowned out the voice.

Then his mind began to clear. He knew he was in a helicopter, that someone was talking about him, and they'd noticed he was waking up.

"There will be some initial disorientation and minor dizziness from the drug, Detective Schaefer, but that will pass," the voice said. Schaefer blinked and saw that a man in a U.S. Army dress uniform was kneeling over him—an officer. A captain, to be exact. The man looked genuinely concerned— which Schaefer didn't believe for a minute.

He was, he realized, lying on a stretcher aboard a military transport copter—he couldn't be sure what kind from here, with the pilot's compartment curtained off. The captain was probably a doctor, and Schaefer was now awake enough to spot the medical insignia—yes, an army doctor.

Schaefer turned to look to either side. Two other men were crouched nearby—more medical personnel, in whites rather than military garb. Two others, soldiers who looked like guards, sat farther back.

And at his feet sat General Philips.

Schaefer stared at the general for a moment.

He had dealt with Philips before, when those things from outer space had come prowling the Big Apple. Philips was a bastard, no question about it, but he wasn't such a robot as Smithers or the others. Schaefer's brother Dutch had actually liked Philips, and Schaefer himself had seen signs of humanity in the old warhorse.

"Seems like I have fewer legal rights than I thought," Schaefer said. His voice was weak and husky at first; he paused to clear his throat. "Maybe I'm just a dumb cop, General, but isn't kidnapping still illegal in this country? Not to mention murder."

Philips glowered at Schaefer.

He hated dragging civilians into this, especially unwilling ones, but when he'd been called back, after those months of inaction, and had seen what they'd left him to work with, he'd known he was going to need help.

His experts had all been reassigned; research had been stopped dead. Colonel Smithers and his men had been working counterespionage and had been pulled off that and put back under Philips's command just the night before. Captain Lynch's team was still intact, but they'd mostly been marking time, training in marksmanship and demolitions and unarmed combat and not learning a damned thing about the enemy they were supposed to fight.

Because with the researchers gone, nobody in the government *knew*, really knew, anything about the aliens. They'd given him all the staff he asked for, all the authority to call in any help he wanted, and the only person Philips had been able to think of who did know anything, and who could be located on short notice, was Schaefer.

They needed Schaefer. The fate of the whole goddamn world could depend on this man.

And Schaefer wasn't cooperating.

"Don't talk to me about the law, Schaefer," the general retorted. "Some things transcend Man's laws."

Schaefer's eyes narrowed. "And some things don't, General, and who appointed you God's judge and jury, anyway? Those goons of yours blew away two citizens back there!"

"Two citizens who were selling cocaine and who had just helped murder four cops, Schaefer," Philips replied. "I didn't authorize Smithers and his boys to kill them, but don't try to tell me you really give a damn about what happened to Baby or Arturo or Reggie."

Philips wasn't happy about how Smithers had handled matters, but he didn't want to let Schaefer know; this wasn't the time or place to argue about it.

"You know all their names?" Schaefer said. "Hey, I'm impressed."

Much as he hated to admit it, he *was* slightly impressed—he hadn't known Reggie's name himself, nor that Rawlings and the others were definitely dead.

Baby and her friends had had it coming, then— but still, they should have had their fair chance. Arturo had gone down shooting, but Baby and Reggie had been defenseless; they shouldn't have died.

"I do my homework," Philips said. In fact, he'd been cramming desperately ever since the phone call had come.

He held up a manila folder. "For example, I read up on you, Schaefer. You grew up in Pennsylvania, you're good with languages—fluent in Russian and French, picked up some German and Spanish on the streets." The Russian was a lucky break, Philips thought, but he didn't say so. "Joined the NYPD in 1978, made detective in '86. We've got your military records, your department file, hell, we've got your marks from grade school, right back to kindergarten—I notice you got 'needs improvement' for 'works and plays well with others' for three years straight. It looks like you haven't changed all that much since, but I guess we'll just have to put up with you."

"No, you won't," Schaefer said. "You don't need to put up with anything. You can just land this contraption and let me off."

"No, we can't." Philips leaned forward. "I thought Smithers told you, Schaefer. We need you."

"Why?" Schaefer started to sit up, then thought better of it as a wave of dizziness from the aftereffects of the drugs swept over him. "I seem to remember you and your boys telling me to stay the hell out of it when those things came to play in New York—in my town. Now they're making trouble somewhere else, and you want me to get involved?

Why? Maybe it's Washington this time, and you're afraid some senator's going to wind up as a trophy?"

"You know they're back," Philips said. It wasn't a question.

"Of *course* I know they're back!" Schaefer said, sitting up and ignoring the dizziness this time. "For God's sake, General, do you really think I'm as stupid as that? What the hell else would you want *me* for?"

"You're right, God damn you," Philips said. "They *are* back, and that's why we want you."

"So where are they, that you can't just ignore them? Who are they killing this time? Why should *I* care?"

"I wouldn't have brought you in if it weren't absolutely essential to national security," Philips said.

"Christ, it *is* Washington, isn't it?" Schaefer said. "Well, if it is, you can all go fuck yourselves . . ."

Philips shook his head. He'd forgotten how quick Schaefer could be, that despite his looks he wasn't just muscle, but this time he'd got it wrong.

"Not Washington," he said, cutting Schaefer off. "It's not body counts we're worried about this time. It's their technology."

Schaefer frowned.

He didn't get it. Sure, it would be nice to have the gadgets those creatures used, but the good ol' U.S. of A. had gotten along just fine without them for a couple of centuries now. "Why is it suddenly so urgent to capture their technology?" he asked.

"No," Philips said. "That's not it. Not exactly. It's not capturing anything that we need you for."

"Then what the hell is it?"

"Making sure their technology *isn't* captured."

Schaefer stared at Philips.

Schaefer was certain that if it was Americans who captured some of the alien gadgets the general would be turning cartwheels. So it wasn't Americans he was worried about. Who, then?

There must be a spaceship down in some hostile country somewhere. That was the only explanation that made sense.

But even that didn't make *much* sense. The things only hunted in hot climates. Somehow, Schaefer couldn't see a bunch of Iraqi or Somali camel jockeys, or Amazon tribesmen, figuring out how to copy a starship's main drive. "Where the hell *are* they, this time?" he demanded.

Philips made a face, as if there were a bad taste in his mouth.

"Siberia," he said.

11

Lieutenant Ligacheva watched out the window of the military transport plane as the lights of Moscow slowly faded in the distance.

General Ponomarenko had thought he was punishing her by sending her back to Assyma, she was certain. He had almost said as much. Sending her back to the cold and the darkness and the monster that had slain her men—of course that was a punishment, was it not?

If the general thought so, then the general was a fool—at least in that regard.

This was no punishment. She was a *soldier*, something that Ponomarenko seemed to find impossible to believe, and a soldier's first priority was duty. Assyma was unquestionably where her duty lay. Assyma was where the men she had worked with for the past two months were still in danger from whatever was out there on the ice.

She was a soldier, sworn to defend her people, and those people at Pumping Station #12 were her people. Moscow had sent them out there and forgotten them—watching the pipeline was just another necessary but worthless job that had to be done, and the men sent to do it were nothing to their commanders back in the capital.

But they were everything to Ligacheva. Ponomarenko couldn't have stopped her from returning if he had tried; it would merely have taken her longer.

She turned her gaze to what lay ahead of the plane. She could see nothing out there but haze and darkness. Somewhere ahead of her was Assyma. Somewhere out there were her home, her post, her duty—and whatever it was that had slaughtered her squad.

She stared into the darkness and wondered what Galyshev and the others she had left behind were doing about the killer out there in the night.

At that moment, in the science station of the complex at Assyma, Galyshev was leaning over Sobchak, once again angrily demanding answers to the questions he needed to ask, questions he couldn't put clearly into words, questions that Sobchak understood anyway—and questions that Sobchak, much as he wanted to, couldn't answer.

"I tell you, Galyshev, I don't *know* what happened to the squad," Sobchak repeated. "You were there when the villagers brought the lieutenant in, and when they came to pick her up—you know as much as I do."

"No," Galyshev said. "*You* spoke to Moscow on the radio. They asked for *you*."

"But they didn't tell me anything! They just asked questions."

"They didn't tell you *anything*?"

"Only that they had flown the lieutenant straight to Moscow for questioning, they told me that much, and they said they'd send more men back with her, but that's *all they said*, I swear it!"

"That's not good enough!" Galyshev raged, slamming a gloved fist against the concrete wall. "*You* sent for Lieutenant Ligacheva, Sobchak! *You* told her about something out there, she took the squad to investigate it, and *no one came back*! Now, tell me what you sent her there to find! What's *out* there, Sobchak?"

"I don't know! I told you, I had seismic readings, radiation readings, and I sent her to *find out* what caused them! I *don't know*!"

"You don't just *lose* an army squad, Sobchak, not even out here," Galyshev insisted. "They had the truck, the truck had a radio, they had plenty of weapons and fuel. What *happened* to them?"

"I don't know!" Sobchak was almost weeping. "The authorities wouldn't tell me anything! All they told me was that the whole squad was gone, and the lieutenant was on her way to Moscow!"

"Gone? How, gone? Where, gone? Are they dead, are they kidnapped?"

Sobchak turned up his empty hands and shook his head. "*Ya nye znayu*—I don't know," he said again.

Galyshev glared at him. Sobchak was sweating, but he kept it so warm in this room of his that Galyshev couldn't be sure whether that was nervousness or just because Sobchak was overheated.

If Sobchak got really scared, he might start babbling or break down completely; that wouldn't help. Even through his anger, Galyshev could see that. He tried to force himself to be calm and reasonable.

"Listen, Sobchak," he said. "The men are frightened, and I can't blame them. There's talk of a strike, of shutting down the pumps—tell me something I can use to calm them down, to ease their fears of whatever's out there."

"Out there?" Sobchak asked. He laughed nervously, recovering himself somewhat, and wiped at the sweat on his forehead. "I would be afraid of Moscow, and what they'll do to whoever they choose to blame for this, not of what Ligacheva went to investigate. Yes, there was something out there, something that registered on the seismograph, something hot, something radioactive—but it's *out there*, whatever it is, out in the snow, it's not in here. The walls are concrete, the doors are steel—what are the men scared of, Galyshev, ghosts? Are they children?"

Galyshev's temper snapped. He was a big man, he'd worked his way up from the construction crews that built the pipeline; he grabbed the dirty white lapels of Sobchak's lab coat and lifted. The scientist came up out of his seat and hung in Galyshev's grip like a rag doll.

"Damn you to *hell*, Sobchak!" Galyshev growled. "Locked in here with your papers and your manuals and your meters you haven't *felt* it, but the *rest* of us have!" He shook Sobchak as a terrier shakes a rat. "There's something out there, Sobchak! We all know it, we've sensed it. It's out there, watching and waiting. It took the squad, I know it did—dead or alive I can't say, but it took them, whatever it is. And steel doors or not, it might try for us!"

"You're mad," Sobchak gasped.

Galyshev flung the scientist back into his chair. "Mad?" he said. "Maybe I am. But if I'm not, then there's something out there, and it's not going to stop with the soldiers. Sooner or later, it's coming for all of us!"

"That's ridiculous!" Sobchak said. "Ridiculous! There is something out there, Galyshev, or there was—but it's not some arctic ghost monster come to eat us all in our beds. My best guess is that it's an American plane or satellite, down on the ice."

"Americans?" Galyshev straightened, startled. "What would Americans want *here*?"

"Who knows?" Sobchak replied. "But the impact of a downed plane, a large one, would account for the seismic disturbance. Burning fuel could have been responsible for the heat, and who knows what might have caused the radiation, eh? Isn't something like that far more likely than your ghosts that walk through walls?"

Galyshev considered that. "And the missing soldiers?" he asked.

Sobchak shrugged. "Ambushed by the Americans, perhaps, or caught in an explosion . . ."

Galyshev frowned. "*Was* there an explosion?" He gestured at the seismographs and other equipment.

"Well . . . well, it's hard to be sure," Sobchak said, which Galyshev immediately realized meant there was no evidence of any explosion. "The storm distorted the readings. But there might have been one, I can't tell. A small one."

Galyshev glared at Sobchak. "You believe this?" he demanded.

Sobchak let out his breath in a deep sigh. "I *told* you, Galyshev, I *don't know*. I am a scientist—I believe what I can see, what I can demonstrate, I take nothing on faith. This idea about downed Americans is my best hypothesis, but I have no way to test it, not until the storm stops and Lieutenant Ligacheva returns with more soldiers."

"Very well," Galyshev said, turning away. "I accept that you do not know what is out there, that it might be American spies. You will watch your dials and gauges then, Sobchak, and you will tell me at once anything you learn. And if you speak to the authorities again, or anyone else, you will tell me that, as well. Now, I'll try to calm the men, to get us all back to work."

"Very good," Sobchak said primly as he began reconstructing his customary calm detachment. "Thank you, Galyshev."

Galyshev marched out through the barren ante-room of the scientific station and back down the corridor toward the rest of the complex. After the damp heat of Sobchak's hideaway the cool air of the passage was like a bracing shower, clearing away the fog.

The men wouldn't like this, that the authorities had said nothing. They would be pleased to hear that more soldiers were coming, perhaps less pleased to hear that the cocky young Lieutenant Ligacheva was returning with them—the men liked her well enough, and Galyshev included himself in that, but they still had doubts about her abilities. She was still very young for an officer, and despite her efforts to prove herself any man's equal, she was still a woman, though admittedly perhaps an exceptional one. The men might well have preferred a more experienced, more authoritative officer in charge—and Galyshev wouldn't blame them for it if they did.

As for the rest of it, they might or might not accept Sobchak's guess that it was a crew of downed Americans who were responsible for the squad's disappearance. While it might be the most logical explanation, it didn't *feel* right to him, and Galyshev knew the others would think the same.

He could feel the cold seeping into the corridor through the concrete walls as he walked. He even thought he could hear the wind howling overhead.

Why would Americans venture into this white wasteland, this frozen corner of hell? Americans were soft creatures who lived in warm, easy places like Florida and California; why would they ever leave their sunny homes to come to this cold, bleak land of months-long nights?

It was almost easier to believe in arctic ghosts.

12

Master pipefitter Sergei Yevgenyevich Buyanov was not at all happy to be out in the snow, walking the station's pair of guard dogs.

Ordinarily he wasn't supposed to handle them at all; that had been Salnikov's job. But Salnikov hadn't come back from Sobchak's little errand, so someone had to take the dogs out, and Buyanov had been ordered to do it. He had made the mistake of admitting that he knew something about dogs.

The dogs didn't seem very happy about the state of affairs, either, and it wasn't just the cold— Buyanov was certain of that. Instead of trotting along as they usually did, sniffing at anything interesting, they hugged the station's walls and seemed to be constantly whining, heads down, or else staring out into the icy gloom of the arctic night and making unhappy noises in their throats.

At first Buyanov had thought it was just him,

that the dogs didn't like him, that they missed Salnikov, but when they didn't improve, and it sank in
that they always both looked into the darkness in
the same direction, he reconsidered.

There was something somewhere *out there* that
they didn't like.

But there wasn't anything out there, Buyanov
told himself. It was quiet and clear. The storm had
ended, at least for the moment—everyone who had
been here for more than a single winter seemed to
agree that this was probably just a lull and they
could expect howling winds and blinding snow to
come sweeping back down on them at any time, but
right now the air was calm—so cold and still that it
seemed almost solid, as if all the world were
encased in crystal.

Did the dogs sense a new storm coming?

That couldn't be it—there were storms here all
the time, and Buyanov had never heard of the dogs
being spooked like this before.

There had been all those stories about the
missing squad, about ghosts or monsters or some
crazy American commando mission, but Buyanov
hadn't believed any of that—and he didn't *see* anything. He stared repeatedly in the direction that
seemed to worry the dogs and couldn't make out
anything but snow, ice, and the overcast sky.

"What the hell's the *matter* with you?" he
demanded, tugging at the leashes as the dogs
crouched, staring out into the wilderness. "There's
nothing out there!"

Just then a puff of wind swept down at them
from the nearby hilltop; snow swirled around
Buyanov's boots. As if that had shattered the stillness gusts and eddies began to appear everywhere.

That new storm was definitely coming, Buyanov decided, and might break any moment. The storm was coming, and he wanted to get back inside, where it was warm, where he wouldn't have to worry about these crazy dogs, and where he wouldn't find himself half believing children's stories about snow demons or ghosts. Next thing you know, he told himself, I'll start believing Baba Yaga's out there, coming in her chicken-legged house to snatch me up for her stewpot.

"Come on!" he said angrily, giving both the leashes another yank.

The dogs didn't move. The big female growled, deep in her throat. This wasn't just worry, Buyanov knew—he did know *something* about dogs, or he wouldn't have spoken up and wouldn't have been given this duty. That was a serious warning, that growl, and Buyanov knew it. That wasn't playing, or any sort of low-level threat; that was a "back off right now or I'll rip your throat out" growl, nothing halfhearted or playful about it. If any dog had ever growled at Buyanov like that, he'd have backed down immediately.

She wasn't growling at him, though. She was growling at something *out there*.

"There's nothing out there," Buyanov repeated, baffled and frightened. "Just the wind."

The dog barked angrily, once, her hot breath a dense cloud in the cold air. The wind picked up just then, and snow sprayed up from the hillside, glittering white in the light from one of the station's few windows, like a flurry of diamond dust.

The storm *was* coming, no doubt about it, and coming fast. Buyanov realized suddenly that that eerie stillness must have been the calm before the storm that people spoke about. Wind roared in the distance.

"Come *on*," he said, pulling at the leash.

The big dog jerked back, and the leather strap slipped from Buyanov's glove. The dog immediately charged up the hillside, her legs churning through the drifts as she bounded away into the darkness and swirling snow.

"*No!*" Buyanov shouted. "Come back, damn it!"

The dog didn't come back, and by the time the echoes of his own shout had died away Buyanov couldn't hear her anymore over the mounting howl of the wind.

"God damn it," Buyanov said as he dragged the other dog growling and yapping around the final corner to the door. The dog planted his feet, but Buyanov was bigger and stronger, and with just the one dog now he could rely on brute force to haul the animal to the door.

He shoved the heavy steel door open and caught a faceful of warm, damp air that felt like a foretaste of heaven; the entryway was unlit, but light spilled out from somewhere farther inside, tempting Buyanov.

He did not yield. He had to track down and recover the other dog.

"Get in there," he said, shoving the other dog inside. Then he flung in the leash and slammed the door, shutting the dog inside and himself outside in the storm.

He would have to be careful when he returned, he reminded himself, and make sure that the stupid cur wasn't waiting there to lunge out the instant the door opened again.

Right now, though, he intended to find the first dog and haul her back.

"I should let you freeze, you stupid bitch," he muttered as he located the dog's tracks and began following them up the hillside. The wind was fierce now, already approaching gale force; he shielded his eyes with one gloved hand, trying to see clearly through wind and snow and night. He would have to move quickly if he didn't want to lose the trail—drifting snow would cover it in minutes, he was sure.

"When I find you, I'll . . ." he began, but then he stopped; he couldn't think of any appropriate vengeance that he would dare take on Salnikov's dogs. "By God, I'll do *something,* you miserable . . ." He peered into the darkness; he was over the hilltop now.

Something slammed into him, something big and soft and heavy that hit him *hard.* He toppled backward into the snow and felt the cold crystals spray into his boots and gloves and collar, felt the icy hardness of the ground as he landed flat on his back.

He blinked, clearing the snow from his eyes, and saw what had hit him.

His missing dog lay on his chest, her face mere centimeters from his own. Her eyes were blank and staring, and blood was trickling from her open mouth.

"What . . ." He sat up, enough adrenaline pumping through his veins that the dead dog's weight might as well not even have been there. As he rose the dog rolled down to lie lifelessly across his legs.

Blood was everywhere, on his coat and his boots and his leggings and thickly matted on the dog's fur.

The dog had been gutted. Something had ripped open her belly in two long slices, side by side.

"What could have *done* this?" he asked, staring.

Then he realized that the dog had not jumped on him; the corpse had been *flung*. What could have thrown it with such force?

He looked up, and there they were, three of them, standing in the snow, watching him.

They were bigger than humans; the shortest was well over two meters. They were shaped more or less like men, but their faces were hidden by metal masks, their hands ended in claws. They wore no coats, despite the cold, and bristled with unfamiliar weaponry. Their skin was yellow, where it showed; their hair, if it *was* hair, was worn in long, decorated, snakelike braids that flapped eerily in the wind.

"My God," Buyanov whispered.

They stood, motionless, watching him, for a long moment. Buyanov stared back.

Gradually sense returned. These, Buyanov realized, were undoubtedly the snow devils, the arctic ghosts, that had taken the soldiers. When he understood that, he expected to die within seconds of that first sight.

Then he saw that they weren't approaching him. They weren't killing him. They were just *standing* there.

They had gutted the dog, but she had undoubtedly attacked them. They had almost certainly killed or captured the missing soldiers, but they, too, had presumably intruded where they weren't welcome.

Buyanov hadn't done anything to anger them, had he? They were going to let him go, he told himself; that was why they hadn't killed him. He hadn't meant them any harm, so they were letting him go.

He scrambled to his feet, shoving the dead dog aside, and backed slowly away.

They didn't move.

Buyanov bowed awkwardly. "Thank you, my lords," he said, stumbling over the unfamiliar pre-Soviet words. He had never before in his life called anyone "lord," had never heard the term used except in satires and historical dramas, but what else could he say to these creatures, these ice demons?

He turned, trying to decide whether to walk or run. He took two short steps, trying to maintain some trace of dignity, then glanced back.

The nearest of the demons took a step closer. It moved swiftly, with an appearance of immense power. Its face was hidden by its mask, unreadable, but Buyanov read hostility in the way it stood, the way it moved; he ran.

As he neared the station he began shouting, "Open the door! Help! Help me!" He slammed into the door, too hysterical to work the heavy hatchlock mechanism at first, and pounded on it with both fists.

A moment later the door swung open, and two worried faces peered out at him.

"Sergei!" someone said. "What happened?"

"We saw the dog roaming the corridors," another said.

Buyanov staggered in, and the larger of the two men caught him as he fell, exhausted from his panicky run.

"Get that door closed," the man holding Buyanov called to the other. "It must be sixty below outside!"

"Anatoli," the other man said as he slammed the door, "look! What's that on his coat?"

"Looks like frozen blood," the man holding Buyanov said. "Sergei, what *happened*?"

"Devils," Buyanov gasped. "Devils on the ice— I've seen them, Dmitri!"

The other two exchanged worried glances.

"We've got to warn the oth—" Buyanov began.

He was interrupted by a loud booming as something slammed into the door from outside.

"What was *that*?" Anatoli shouted.

Then all three men froze at the sound of tearing metal. An instant later the gleaming tip of a jagged blade punched through the door.

"But that door is *steel*," Anatoli said. "Ten centimeters of steel!"

All three knew that to be true; the door was a massive slab of solid metal, designed to withstand the mightiest storm—or the explosion of the pipeline itself.

It didn't seem to matter; the jagged blade sliced down through the door slowly, sawing back and forth, like a knife through hard cheese.

"My God!" Dmitri said.

"Warn the others!" Buyanov said. He rolled off Dmitri's knees, caught himself against the wall with one hand, and started to get to his feet.

As he did the ruined door slammed open, and there were those *things*. Buyanov moaned.

"Devil!" Anatoli said.

Then, without warning, moving faster than human eyes could follow, the foremost of the three creatures rammed a spear through Anatoli's chest. Anatoli crumpled; with his lung pierced he couldn't even manage a dying scream.

For an instant everyone remained frozen, Anatoli hunched over the blade that had killed him, the other two staring in shock.

Then the initial shock passed.

"Bastards!" Dmitri shouted. He ran for the nearest alarm box.

One of the creatures ran after him, moving inhumanly fast, so fast Buyanov could not properly follow the motion; as Dmitri's hand reached for the alarm handle the thing's hand slammed down on the top of the Russian's head.

Dmitri staggered and fell to his knees, still reaching for the alarm handle. Buyanov watched, still too astonished and terrified to move.

The thing swung its other hand back, and two curving, crooked blades snapped into place, extending from its wrist past its clenched fist.

Still holding Dmitri's head with one hand, the creature plunged the pair of curved blades into Dmitri's back.

Dmitri convulsed, jerking wildly, then collapsed limply into death—but in his final spasm his hand closed on the alarm handle and yanked it down.

Buyanov saw all that just before a taloned, yellow-skinned hand smashed across his face, knocking him to the floor. He looked up and screamed.

The last thing he saw was the approaching sandal as the thing set one foot on his face; then the creature leaned its full weight on Sergei Yevgenyevich Buyanov and crushed his skull as if it were the shell of an annoying beetle.

13

Galyshev had decided to pay another call on Sobchak, and was just stepping into the geologist's workroom when the alarm sounded.

The superintendent looked up, startled.

"What the hell is *that*?" he demanded.

"An alarm," Sobchak said.

"Why?" Galyshev asked sharply. "Something wrong with the pipeline?"

"Nothing that shows on my equipment," Sobchak said, looking around at the ranked gauges. "But I've lost the feed from the sensors at the east door."

"Something's breaking in over there?" Galyshev demanded, tensing.

"I don't know," Sobchak said, staring at the meters. "I can't tell."

"Well, then I'll find out for myself!" Galyshev

turned and charged out of the room, heading for the passage back to the main part of the complex.

Sobchak watched Galyshev go, then looked at the equipment again.

He didn't have any real surveillance equipment—this was science, not the KGB—but when this monitoring station had been set up they'd had the possibility of accidents, or sabotage, in mind. There were thermosensors and barometers and rem-counters and even microphones scattered through the entire complex, along with the seismic monitors. The theory had been that if the pipeline burst, or a fire started, the station's scientists would be able to track the effects through heat, pressure, radiation, and sound.

Sobchak reached over and turned on all the interior monitors, one by one. Last of all he turned on the speaker for the microphones in the east corridor.

He immediately turned the volume down; the screams were deafening.

"My God," he said. He looked at the other readings, trying to understand.

Sobchak judged that something big and hot had come in through the east door and was moving down the corridor, deeper into the station—the temperature and barometric pressure at the sensors nearest the door were dropping steadily, as if the door was open or even gone, but at the next set the temperature was *higher* than before.

And the radioactivity levels in the east corridor were running about twice what they should be—still harmless, but inexplicable.

The screams, too, were inexplicable—and terrifying.

Sobchak was a man of science. He didn't

believe in arctic ghosts. All the same, he got up and closed the door of his workroom, and locked it.

"To keep in the heat," he told himself. "That's all, to keep in the heat."

He looked around and noticed that he'd left his coat and boots out in the anteroom—he didn't like to have them in the workroom; the equipment was packed in so tightly that they got in the way. He didn't open the door to retrieve them, though. They could wait out there.

In the main station there were men milling about in the common room, unsure what to do, as Galyshev burst from the tunnel.

"Sir, what's going on?" someone called. "What's happening? Why the alarm?"

"Something's broken in the east door," Galyshev called. "We're going to find out who it is!"

The men glanced at one another uneasily.

"But, sir . . ."

"We're not soldiers . . ."

"We're still men, aren't we?" Galyshev demanded. "And there are guns in the armory, aren't there?"

"Armory?"

The glances the men exchanged now were considerably more hopeful.

"We may not be trained soldiers," Galyshev said, "but we can still fight when our home is invaded!" He marched down the corridor to the soldiers' barracks, and after a brief hesitation the others followed him.

Lieutenant Ligacheva had not bothered to lock it before leading her squad out on their fatal investigation. The squad's weapons were gone, no one had recovered them from the ice, but the reserves were

still there, and moments later a dozen men were
marching down the east corridor with AK-74s in
their hands. Galyshev had taken a quick roll call as
he handed out weapons and knew that three men
were missing—Sergei Buyanov, Dmitri Vesnin, and
Anatoli Shvernik.

No one present admitted to sounding the
alarm; presumably one of those three had.

"There was nothing on the radio or the tele-
type?" Galyshev asked as they marched. "Nothing
to warn us some sort of attack might be coming?"

"Nothing at all," Shaporin replied.

"That bothers me . . ." Galyshev began.

Then they turned the final corner, and a blast
of icy wind from the ruined door struck them. It
wasn't the wind that made Galyshev halt dead in
his tracks and stop speaking in midsentence,
though.

It was the blood.

Blood was spattered all over the floor and one
wall, great splashes of blood, still wet.

"What happened here?" Galyshev demanded.

There was no answer.

"Where are the bodies?" Shaporin asked from
just behind. "Whose blood is it?"

"It couldn't just be paint?" someone asked from
farther back.

Galyshev shook his head. "It's not paint." He
studied the floor, the patterns of red, the drops and
smears . . .

"They went down there," he said, jerking the
barrel of his gun. "Toward the pipeline." He flipped
off the safety. "Come on!"

Sure enough, a thin trail of drops of blood led into the tunnel to the maintenance areas.

"What's *in* there?" Rublev asked. "What did this?"

"I don't know," Galyshev said, "and I don't care. Are you coming with me or not?"

Rublev still hesitated.

"Come on, Rublev," Shaporin said. "You think it's monsters in there?"

"More likely Chechen guerrillas," Leskov, the practical joker in the bunch, said. "After all, it's only what, two thousand miles from Chechnya to the Yamal Peninsula? If no one told them the war was over, it might've taken them this long to get here!"

A few of the men grinned, but no one laughed— that blood on the wall was too fresh.

"It's probably American saboteurs," Galyshev said seriously. "Whoever or whatever it is, you think these won't handle the job?" He hefted the AK-74.

The men still hesitated.

"Well, *I'm* going," Galyshev said. "There are three men missing, and maybe they aren't all dead, and if we hurry maybe they'll stay that way." He turned and marched down the side tunnel.

Reluctantly, first Shaporin, then Leskov, and finally the others followed him. Rublev came last.

The little corridor ended in a large open space, a maintenance area under the pipeline. The chamber was intended to give easy access to any part of the pipeline, from the huge valves to the immense pumping equipment at the north end; it ran some sixty meters end to end, almost the full length of the underground portion of the station, and was a good fifteen meters wide. Thick concrete pillars were spaced along the room's length, one every ten meters or so. The oil-spattered floor was poured concrete, sloping slightly to improve drainage, while the walls on either side were concrete block to a height of about three meters. Above those walls a complex maze of steel struts and girders wove overhead, supporting and steadying the immense pipe, and Galyshev had never been sure what the walls up there, hidden behind that framework, looked like.

Regulations required that this entire area be kept clear, so in a crowded, uncomfortable station this huge open space remained virtually empty—and almost unlit. Galyshev reached for the switch at the end of the corridor and flipped it up; three dim work lights came on, but most of the cavernous chamber remained dark.

There should have been more, he knew; they must have burned out. He'd want to do something about that later, during the next round of maintenance.

He stared out into the dimness, scanning the immense chamber for his enemy, whoever it might be; the AK-74 was ready in his hands.

Nothing moved, anywhere that he could see. There were no intruders, nothing out of place. He heard a faint dripping, but that wasn't unusual; not only did the lubricant from the pumps sometimes leak, but the temperature differential between the station's air and the pipeline itself often produced heavy condensation on the pipe.

He glanced up at the pipeline, more out of habit than concern, and froze.

"Holy Mary," he said.

Not all of the spots on the floor, Galyshev realized, were water or oil.

Three headless corpses were dangling by their ankles from the steel framework overhead, dangling and dripping blood into puddles that were slowly oozing down across the floor into the waiting drains.

"So much for finding them alive," Leskov said, with no trace of humor in his voice.

"But who killed them?" Shaporin asked. "And where'd the killers go?"

"There," Galyshev said, pointing. "Rublev, you did your rounds?"

"Yes," Rublev said, trying to see where Galyshev was pointing.

"See the boiler-room door?"

Rublev and the others looked. The boiler plant was just the other side of the maintenance area, closed off by a simple wooden door, a door that was supposed to be kept closed at all times. Whoever had the duty of making the daily security round was supposed to check that door.

"But that was closed!" Rublev protested. "I tried it myself!"

"I'm sure it was," Galyshev said. "Come on."

"But there aren't any lights on in there," Shaporin said as the group began advancing across the concrete.

"I've heard that the Americans use infrared goggles to see in the dark," Leskov said. Galyshev glanced over at him, expecting the comment to be turned into a joke, but Leskov wasn't smiling.

Galyshev remembered who had had watch duty in the boiler room that shift—Dmitri Vesnin, Leskov's best friend. Vesnin had presumably gone to see what was happening at the east door, and now his body was one of the three dangling in the maintenance area.

"Americans?" Shaporin said. "You think Americans would hang them upside down like that?"

"Who else could it be?" Leskov asked.

"Or *what* else could it be," Rublev said. "How could it be anything human? How long would it take to climb up there and hang them up like that?" He gestured with the barrel of his weapon.

"Let's take a look in there and find out," Leskov said, taking a step toward the boiler plant.

"Whoever did this may still be in there, or they may not," Galyshev said, moving along with Leskov. "You wait here—cover me."

"The others can cover us both," Leskov said. "Those were my friends."

"Mine, too," Galyshev said. "Come on, then."

Side by side, the two men advanced across the maintenance area, stalking as if the boiler room were the lair of some dangerous beast—which, Galyshev thought, it might very well be. He had talked bravely about how there were no monsters out there on the ice, but he knew they weren't all *that* far from the old nuclear testing ground on Novaya Zemlya, and visions of horribly mutated polar bears were lurking somewhere in the back of his mind.

Sobchak had said something about higher-than-normal radiation levels back when all this trouble first started, Galyshev remembered that all too well. The scientists all said that the stories of radioactive mutants were nonsense, bad American science fiction—but the scientists had lied before or been wrong before.

And why would any human being hang those corpses up like that? It *had* to be some sort of beast!

He crept up to one side of the door, while Leskov took a position at the other. Galyshev waved to Leskov to wait, then leaned over and slid one hand through the door, groping for the light switch.

"They'd have an advantage with the light behind me," he whispered to Leskov. "I need to *see* them."

Leskov nodded.

Galyshev's fingers found the switch. He tensed, braced himself—then flicked the switch and burst through the door, AK-74 ready.

It took him a moment to understand what he saw.

The door opened on a short passageway, a meter or so long, that led into the main boiler room. That boiler room was not well lit, even with the four ceiling lights on; it was a shadowy place of hissing pipes, black dust, and the orange glow from the burners.

This was the heart of the heating system for the entire complex—here oil was burned to boil water into steam, which was circulated through a network of pipes and radiators to every inhabited portion of Station #12. The oil came straight from the fields, so it was heavy, dirty stuff, and despite the chimneys and blowers soot seeped out into the boiler plant, covering everything with black grit.

The room was sweltering hot, of course, despite the biting cold outside the station. This heat radiated off the main boiler in waves of rippling air. The metal sides of the boiler were too hot to touch—new workers arriving at the station sometimes put themselves in the infirmary with second-degree burns while discovering this.

Galyshev had been working in Assyma for years; he would no more have touched the boiler than he would have thrust his bare hand into live coals.

It took him a moment, therefore, to realize that he really did see three big, man-shaped creatures leaning up against the boiler, their backs pressed tight to the unbearably hot metal.

He couldn't shoot them, he realized; his fire would hit the boiler. The metal walls were thick, but the boiler was old, and was designed to hold pressure *in*, not to keep bullets out. It might explode if he shot at it.

These things were unquestionably the killers, though. They held things like spears, there were jagged blades on their wrists . . .

And they weren't human at all, he realized. Not only could they press up against metal heated to 120 degrees Celsius without being burned, but they were huge, their skin was yellowish, their nails black and hard and pointed, like claws. They wore strange metal masks that hid their faces completely, while elsewhere much of their inhuman flesh was exposed.

They not only weren't burned, they seemed to relish the heat.

"My God," Galyshev said as it sank in just what he was seeing.

The three masked faces turned to look at him. Something moved—not one of the creatures themselves, but something on the shoulder of the one nearest Galyshev, something humped and black that lifted up and pivoted to point at him.

Three red dots roved briefly before settling onto Galyshev's face.

A weapon, Galyshev realized, and he started to duck, to point his own weapon, but the blue-white fireball tore his head off before he had had time to fully react.

Leskov had not yet looked into the room, though he had been tempted upon seeing how Galyshev was staring; he was holding himself back, staying in reserve, letting Galyshev take the lead here. Galyshev was the superintendent, after all.

Then something flashed blue-white, momentarily blinding Leskov. Galyshev's AK-74 stuttered briefly as the superintendent's finger squeezed the trigger in a dying spasm, and when Leskov could see again Galyshev's headless corpse was falling to the floor.

Leskov let out a wordless scream of rage and fear and swung himself into the doorway, firing wildly.

He never even saw them. He saw a blur, and then felt the hot shocking pain of a blade ripping through his belly, and then Leskov died, falling beside Galyshev, the AK-74 spraying bullets across the boiler-room ceiling as he toppled backward.

On the other side of the maintenance area the others watched in horror. They saw the blue-white flash, saw Galyshev and Leskov fall, but they didn't see the enemy, didn't see what had killed the two.

"What happened to them?" Shaporin asked. He raised his voice and shouted, "Who are you? Who's in there? Why are you *doing* this?"

No one answered.

"I don't like this," Rublev said. "I'm no soldier.

I'm getting out of here." He began creeping backward up the corridor.

Then there was another blue-white flash, this one tearing across the full width of the maintenance area, and Shaporin crumpled to the concrete, his chest blown apart. Rublev turned and ran.

None of the men ever got a clear look at their attackers; the things moved too fast, the light was poor. A few fired their weapons wildly into the darkness, hoping to hit something, but without effect.

Five more men died before they could even attempt to flee; Rublev was the only one to make it as far as the main corridor. He didn't turn to see if anyone was pursuing him, didn't turn to see what had happened to his comrades.

He didn't see the spear until it had punched through his body. Then he glimpsed the barbed, red-coated blade for only an instant before he died.

Rublev's body hung limply on the spear for a moment as the creature looked around, scanning the corridor for any further sign of life.

Then it flung the corpse aside and returned to the warmth of the boiler plant.

14

James Theodore Ridgely, U.S. ambassador to the United Nations, had never trusted the Russians.

He hadn't trusted them when they called themselves Soviets and preached their Communist bullshit about historic inevitability, and he didn't trust them now when they called themselves Russians again and talked about the brotherhood of nations.

He didn't mind if they knew it, either—in fact, he took pride in thinking he was doing his bit to let the Russkies know they weren't fooling everybody. That might, he thought, help keep them in line.

And someone, going by the intelligence report he'd just received, was sure as hell out of line *now*. Four hundred percent increase in background radiation in the Assyma region on the Yamal Peninsula? Huge localized rise in temperature? That didn't happen by itself, or because some factory worker dropped a canister.

He had had to check a map to be sure just where the hell the Yamal Peninsula *was*. Northwestern Siberia, on the Arctic Ocean—not that you were ever likely to see any open seawater *that* far north! That was hundreds of miles from the border with the Norwegian part of Lapland, thousands of miles from the Bering Strait.

The middle of fucking *nowhere*, that's where the Yamal Peninsula was.

So of course this Assyma place was an oil field. One of the coldest, most barren places on Earth, colder than the North Pole itself, and the Russians were pumping thousands of barrels of high-grade oil out of the ground there.

Ridgely sometimes, in his more profanely imaginative moments, thought that God had been playing games when He decided where to put petroleum deposits. It seemed as if He had gone looking for the most miserable, useless places He could possibly put the stuff—godforsaken deserts, icy hellholes, underwater . . . maybe God just didn't *like* oil, so He tried to put it in places where He wouldn't have to look at it, places that belonged to the most unpleasant people available.

So, of course, the Yamal Peninsula was just filthy with the stuff.

Oil wasn't radioactive, though. That wasn't any oil spill or wellhead fire that the satellites had spotted. And there weren't supposed to be any nuclear power plants anywhere around there.

There probably weren't any power plants. Building a nuclear plant in the middle of an oil field a thousand miles from the nearest city—now, *that* would be *way* up there on the stupidity lists. It was a safe bet even the Russians weren't that dumb. Ridgely wouldn't have put it past the Iranians or the French, but the Russians knew better.

The flare-up was too far inland to be a grounded submarine with reactor trouble. The Russians still had plenty of subs cruising the arctic, but there wouldn't be any reactor leaks a hundred miles from the coast.

Not natural, not a power plant, not a sub—that left weapons.

It had to be weapons, and messing around with nuclear weapons there was definitely out of line. The Russians swore they were disassembling nukes, not building them, and that sort of radiation and heat spill could equally well have come from an accident in either assembly or disassembly, but all the official disassembly was going on in the *south*, not way the hell up in the arctic.

So somebody was up to something.

Ridgely wasn't entirely convinced it was the boys in Moscow. It could just as easily have been one of the various loony factions that were causing trouble over there, the nationalists or the leftover Commies or the local mafias, but whoever it was, Moscow had to know about it, and they should have passed on a quiet word or two to someone, just so no one would get too upset.

They should have told someone, and most likely, they should have told *him*.

Ridgely had gotten a few sub-rosa reports from his Russian counterparts in his day, and had now and then passed them along a few little warnings of his own. Just because he didn't trust the sneaky bastards was no reason to risk letting the whole

fucking world blow up in his face over some trivial
little misunderstanding.

He hadn't gotten any word on *this* one, though.

He dropped the printout, picked up the phone,
then hesitated.

These were *nukes* they were talking about. This
was the big time. And on the arctic coast, the only
logical place to aim nukes was over the pole at
North America. If this was a bunch of Islamic terrorists or some African government trying to pick
up a little atomic blackmail fodder on the cheap,
those readings would have been down in the Cau-
casus or central Asia somewhere, not in Siberia.

It might be Zhirinovsky's crazies or something,
but by God Moscow should have told them by now;
they'd had a couple of days, and Ridgely hadn't
heard a peep. A phone call just wasn't going to do
an adequate job of expressing American displeasure
at that silence.

This called for a personal visit.

A *public* personal visit.

He picked up the phone after all and punched
the button for his secretary.

"Yes, Ambassador?" she said instantly. Ridgely
smiled. He appreciated competence.

"Steffie, honey," he said, "I'm going to be
paying a little visit on the Russian ambassador at"—
he glanced at the clock—"at about two, I'd say."
That would be after Grigori got back from lunch,
but before he got busy—and if his lunch ran late,
then Ridgely could camp out and make a show of
it. "I think that if some of our friends from the press
happened to come by about then, they might be
interested in what I've got to say to the old boy."

"On or off the record?" Steffie asked.

"Oh, I think this'll be on the record," Ridgely said, leaning back in his chair. "Nothing official, though, just a chat we don't mind having reported."

"Got it, Ambassador," Steffie said. "So is this a *surprise* visit, or should I tell Mr. Komarinets's staff that you're coming?"

Ridgely considered that. He noticed that she didn't bother asking if she should try to make an appointment; Steffie knew her job.

"Make it a five-minute warning, maybe," he said.

"Yes, sir."

Ridgely hung up the phone and smiled a tight little smile of satisfaction.

Those bastards weren't going to get away with anything on *his* watch!

15

My government knows nothing of any clandestine activity of any sort in that area, Mr. Ambassador," Grigori Komarinets had repeated, speaking not to Ridgely but directly into the CNN camera.

General Mavis stood with his hands clasped behind his back as he watched the report on the big TV in the situation room. This Ambassador Komarinets was good, no question—or maybe the folks in Moscow had lied to him, and he honestly didn't know what was going on.

"Meeters," he said, "call someone, make sure Ridgely gets a cookie for helping us out on this—an assignment in Vienna, a shot on Larry King, whatever makes him happy."

"Yessir," Meeters replied. He stood where he was; Mavis hadn't said to call *now*. And there wasn't any hurry; these things were best done discreetly, not making the connection *too* obvious. Mavis glanced at him.

Meeters looked uneasy, preoccupied—but then, why shouldn't he? According to CNN, they might be working up toward World War III.

And they might be, at that, but not the way any of these people thought.

Mavis turned back to the screen and watched for a few seconds more, until CNN cut to a commercial. Then he turned and headed down the corridor toward his office.

Meeters, after an instant's hesitation, followed; when they were out of earshot of the officers still watching the TV, he jogged a few steps to catch up and said, "Excuse me, sir—might I have a word with you?"

Mavis glanced back at the other, then led the way into his office.

"Close the door if you like," he said as he sat down on a corner of his desk. "What's on your mind?"

Meeters stepped in and closed the door. "Sir," he said, "I was there when the preliminary satellite reports came in—I was the one who released that first report, and at the time I was sure someone was hauling warheads out there."

"And?" Mavis said.

"Well, sir, I was wrong," Meeters said. "I've been looking at the technical reports, and I don't think we're seeing missiles out there. The figures don't add up."

Mavis nodded. "You figured that out all by yourself, did you?"

"Yessir," Meeters said. "And if those *aren't* bombs or missiles, then Ambassador Ridgely and the rest could be stirring up a hornet's nest over a threat that doesn't even exist. We might be . . ."

Mavis held up a hand and cut him off. "Stop right there." He stood up. "I like you, Meeters—you're a good man, you take orders but you're not afraid to make decisions. You've got a good brain. And that's why I'm not going to have you arrested and thrown into protective custody."

Meeters blinked. "Sir?"

"All right, that hot spot isn't any Russian missiles," Mavis said. "Think it through, then. There's *something* there, so if it isn't nukes, what is it?"

Meeters looked blank.

"Think, man," Mavis said. "What might it be?"

"I don't know, sir."

"Whatever it is, there's a lot of energy being thrown around, right?"

"Yes, sir . . ."

"Well, then, maybe it's something our weapons people wouldn't mind getting a look at." He decided to go ahead and let Meeters in on it—if he picked up the clues.

"Maybe it's something we've had a shot at before and didn't get. Something you probably heard rumors about, but couldn't get confirmed. Maybe you thought those rumors were bullshit—well, they weren't."

Meeters looked baffled. "I'm not following you, sir," he said.

"Last time we saw something like this was six months ago, in New York," Mavis said.

Meeters looked blank; then his jaw dropped. "Oh, my God," he said, suddenly understanding. "I thought . . . yes, I heard rumors, but I thought it was a hoax or a cover-up."

"No," Mavis said. "It's real."

"But, sir—aliens? A spaceship?"

Mavis nodded. "An entire fucking fleet of spaceships, actually. At least, in New York."

"Then . . . excuse me, sir, but what do we hope to accomplish this time, when they're in Siberia? What's the point of blaming it all on the Russians?"

"The point is to keep the Russians busy, let 'em know we're watching them—and to keep our own people from figuring out what's going on and spreading it all over the news. We don't want anyone to know about these creatures—it'd cause panic if too much got out."

"But these . . . Doesn't the public . . ." Meeters paused, not sure where to begin; the whole issue was too large, so large that he couldn't quite believe the military had a right to keep the public ignorant.

"Listen, Meeters," Mavis said, "I don't know how much you heard about the operation in New York, so let me tell you a few things. These aren't cuddly little E.T.s come to invite us to join the Galactic Brotherhood. They're a bunch of vicious bastards. We don't know for sure why they come here, what they want, or how they'll react to anything we do, but we *do* know that they have technology that makes us look like a bunch of aborigines. If we go ahead and tell everyone yes, we've been visited by monsters from outer space— and yes, they *are* monsters—then we can guess some of the reactions we'll get from the public; we'll have panics and new religions popping up and crazies blaming it on the CIA and people screaming at us for covering up and others saying it's all a hoax. Right now we can't even prove it's *not* a hoax—those things cover their tracks. All that would be bad enough, but what worries us is how *they* would react."

"They?"

"The aliens."

"Oh."

"Because, Meeters, we see three possible outcomes if word gets out that we have these nasty visitors dropping in." He held up one hand and ticked off fingers.

"First, they might not care—they might go on just as they always have. That's arguably the best case all around, though since they do kill people it's not ideal."

He raised a second finger.

"Second, they might just pack up and leave. That means no more killings, but it also means we have no chance of learning any more about them, or about whatever else might be out there waiting for us. We don't like that much. But it still beats the third option."

He raised his third finger.

"Third, they might invade. They might just decide that the cat's out of the bag and there's no more point in subtlety. And if they do, Meeters, we're dead meat."

Meeters frowned. "Sir, the way I heard it," Meeters said, "we *won* in New York."

"More of a draw, at best," Mavis said judiciously. "We didn't capture anything, and we didn't beat them, but they're gone. They went away—but they left because they were done with their visit, not because we really hurt them. And that was on our own territory, with everything in our favor. Those things play *rough*."

"So it's because of that third possibility that we're keeping quiet?"

"That, and other considerations."

"But what if they decide to invade anyway? Shouldn't we be doing something . . . ?"

"We *are,* Meeters." Mavis sat down again. "That's what this whole operation is about. We're trying to get our hands on some of their technology, to see if we can't take a few jumps forward so that if they *do* decide to take over, we stand a fighting chance."

"You said they cover their tracks."

"Sure they do. But they're not infallible. We didn't capture anything in New York or in the other visits we know about—and yes, there have been others—but this time it's not a whole fleet. It looks like a solo, and one that's run into trouble." He pointed in the general direction of the situation room. "That landing in Siberia didn't look planned, Meeters. We might be looking at a shipwreck rather than an invasion, so this could be the best chance we'll ever have. We want whatever we can get that's out there. In fact, we're sending a team in after it— General Philips and a bunch of his boys."

Mavis stood again. "And that's what the cover story is about, Meeters," he said. "If the Russians scream about an intrusion on their territory, we'll just say we were responding to a terrorist threat. Our pal Ridgely just set that up for us, and Komarinets fell right into it by claiming his bosses didn't know anything." He grimaced. "If we get what we're after, great; if we don't, and the Russians don't, because those *things* get their ship

flying again and get away and cover their tracks as
well as usual, we'll live with that, too. If Philips and
his team get killed or captured, well, it's an embarrassment, but they were an embarrassment anyway,
and legally that whole department doesn't even
exist, it's all black budget—we could even claim
they're freelance. The *important* thing here is that
we don't want to wind up with those alien toys in
Russian hands, and not in ours."

That said, he stared at Meeters, awaiting a
reaction.

Meeters stared back, unable to think of a reply;
finally he simply said, "Yessir."

The helicopter pilot called back, "General
Philips? We'll be on the ground in five minutes."

"Good," Philips replied. "Radio ahead, tell
Lynch to have the men ready."

Schaefer snorted. "Lynch," he said. "Good
name. Wouldn't want to let any nasty little details
like the law get in the way."

Philips turned on him angrily. "Damn it,
Schaefer," he said. "I wouldn't have hauled your
ass down here if I didn't think we needed *you*, and
nobody else."

Schaefer glared silently at him. He was tempted
to ask whether they'd ever considered asking
Rasche—after all, Rasche had pulled his own
weight last summer, same as he always did, and
Rasche might still be naive enough, or altruistic
enough, or *something* enough, to have cooperated
with Philips without this much hassle.

He didn't mention Rasche, though, because he
didn't want to give the general any ideas. Rasche

had his own life out there in Oregon, and Schaefer wasn't about to do anything that could screw it up.

"I've got a good team put together," Philips said, "but they've never seen actual *combat* with those things."

"What about all those boys you had on Third Avenue last summer?" Schaefer asked. "Whatever happened to them—they all take early retirement or get hit by the last round of 'Reduction in Force'?"

Philips shook his head. "Firing a few rounds at a spaceship isn't what I had in mind as actual combat. You *know* something about those creatures, Schaefer. You have a feel for the way they think. My men don't."

"Teach 'em."

"We're trying."

"So what are you doing to prepare 'em?" Schaefer asked. "Screening old Godzilla movies?"

"Damn it," Philips shouted, "we're hauling *you* down here to teach 'em!"

"But why should I?"

Philips gritted his teeth and glowered silently at Schaefer for a moment. Schaefer glared back.

"You want the Russians to get their hands on one of those spaceships?" Philips said at last.

"I'm not sure it'd be any worse than *you* getting hold of one," Schaefer retorted.

"Even if it's Zhirinovsky's crew that winds up with those shoulder cannon or with spaceships? Or if some of those starving scientists of theirs sell a few tidbits to the Iranians or the Serbs?"

Schaefer frowned and didn't answer the question. Instead he said, "I'm still having a hard time buying this Siberia shit. General, you say you want me because I know something about what they're like—well, one thing I know is that they hate the cold. So if you're really planning to ship me out to the ass end of nowhere, to look at a spaceship somewhere north of the Arctic Circle, I'll tell you right now that I'm not convinced it's really the same things we're dealing with this time as it was before. Maybe it's some *other* goddamn alien tourists who dropped in on us. Maybe Earth suddenly turned into the trendy watering hole for half the galaxy, and instead of weapons we'll just be picking up a bunch of cosmic beer cans."

"Jesus, you really *work* at being a hard-ass, don't you, Schaefer?" Philips asked. "You look for any reason you can find to make this harder on everybody. You think we're all idiots? You think we didn't check this out, didn't think of the possibility that it's somebody else? Sure, those things like it hot, but they don't like it *radioactive*—the ships in New York didn't leak neutrons when they landed. This one did. And the ones in New York weren't spraying heat around like a fucking furnace, and this one is."

"So it's not the same gang," Schaefer said. "If you can handle one species of alien showing up on our doorsteps, why not two or three?"

"Because everything else fits, Schaefer. So they were in *trouble* when they came down this time. Something was fucked up somewhere. It's the same creatures; it's just how they came down that's different. We think it was a forced landing, Schaefer— maybe a crash. All the stories about the Roswell saucer are a bunch of bull, but this one's real, which means we might have a good chance of getting a look at their technology—if the Russians don't get it first."

"And if they don't blow it all to hell. Remember the one Dutch killed in Central America."

"You think we could forget?" Philips eyed Schaefer thoughtfully. "You still won't help?"

"You haven't said anything to change my mind," Schaefer said. "Why should I care whether we beat the Russians? We beat 'em to the Moon, and all we got out of that was Tang."

Philips nodded. "All right then, screw the patriotism approach," he said. "If you won't work with us because it's best for the country, how about for your family? This team, these men, this whole project, they mean a lot to me. You help them, help *me,* and I'll do what I can to get you some information on your brother."

Schaefer stared silently at him for several long seconds. Then he asked, "If I go along on this little jaunt of yours, you'll tell me what happened to Dutch?"

"I'll try."

Schaefer considered for another long moment, then said, "I'll think about it."

Philips looked at Schaefer's face and decided not to push his luck. He sat back and waited for the chopper to land.

16

The plywood targets were cut to roughly humanoid shape and painted with pictures of the alien predators, but done entirely in a dull blue that was almost invisible in the dimly lit shooting range. Schaefer guessed that this was supposed to make the targets resemble the effects of the things' invisibility field.

It didn't. The invisibility field had made the damn things *invisible,* not just hard to see; with that and how fast they moved, you were lucky to catch so much as a faint shimmer in the air before they ripped your head off.

Schaefer didn't bother mentioning this. Instead he watched silently as the four big men with self-satisfied grins cut loose with heavy-caliber automatic weapons and reduced three of the sheets of plywood to splinters.

The fourth target had one side ripped out, but remained largely intact.

"This team is the elite, Schaefer," Philips said. "Culled from all three services. What do you think?"

"I think you're wasting a lot of good plywood," Schaefer replied.

Philips didn't respond. He had a horrible suspicion that Schaefer was right.

The six men ambled down toward the other end of the range—the shooters to inspect their handiwork, and Schaefer because it seemed to be expected. The four men who were supposed to be his students or teammates carried their weapons with them—that would be a violation of safety rules at an ordinary range, but here it seemed to be expected. Schaefer watched the way the four walked—self-assured, cocky, supremely confident.

Not good. Overconfidence got men killed, and until you'd gone up against your enemy and knew what you were facing, *any* sort of confidence was overconfidence.

"What's the matter, Wilcox?" one of them asked, pointing at the surviving target. "Forget your glasses?"

Wilcox frowned. "Hell, I figured I'd leave something for the *rest* of you, that's all."

Schaefer looked at the target. It had been made with one arm raised in a threatening gesture; the artist had included the wrist blades the aliens used, though he'd gotten the shape of the curve wrong. Given that unless the artist had been there on Third Avenue last summer, he'd never seen one of the creatures, he'd done a damn good job getting as close as he did.

Wilcox had blown away the other side of the target; that hand raised to strike was still there, and Wilcox was standing directly in front of that arm, trading insults with the other men, ignoring the target, ignoring Schaefer.

Too cocky, definitely. If these bozos expected to survive an encounter with those hunters from outer space, they had to learn not to ignore *anything*. Schaefer reached over and gave the target a shove.

It swung around, and that upraised arm slammed into the side of Wilcox's head. He fell sideways at the impact and landed sprawled on the floor.

Philips winced at the sound.

Wilcox didn't drop his weapon, Schaefer noticed. That was good, anyway. The weapon wasn't any sort of rifle or gun Schaefer recognized—he supposed it was some sort of special top-of-the-line equipment.

Schaefer stepped over toward Wilcox. "Guess you didn't expect it to hit back," he said. "Get used to it. These boys play for keeps and follow their own rules."

"Who the hell are *you*?" Wilcox demanded, pointing his weapon at Schaefer's chest. "And give me one good reason I shouldn't blow your damn head off!"

Schaefer stepped forward and to the side, past the muzzle of the gun, so that Wilcox couldn't swing it around to follow. He bent down and offered Wilcox a hand up.

"The name's Schaefer," he said. Wilcox gripped Schaefer's wrist, and a second later was upright again. He transferred his weapon to his left hand and reached out to shake Schaefer's hand . . .

Schaefer had turned away. "As far as that 'blow my head off' business goes—well, son . . ."

Wilcox glared at Schaefer's back in disbelief—the son of a bitch had knocked him down without warning, and now he thought he was too good to shake hands and make up? He hefted the heavy-assault rifle in his left hand, then grabbed the barrel with his right and swung the weapon like a club, aiming for the back of Schaefer's head. Let the arrogant bastard have a taste of his own medicine!

". . . you wouldn't want to *do* that," Schaefer said, ducking under Wilcox's swing—he had clearly expected it. He pivoted on the ball of one foot and brought his fist up under Wilcox's jaw, driving upward from his crouch.

Fist met jaw with a solid thump, and Wilcox went over backward.

"Especially," Schaefer said as he stood over the dazed trooper, "seeing as I'm unarmed."

"All right, Schaefer," Philips said, stepping forward. "You've made your point. Come on, all of you—the briefing room, right now."

It took a moment before anyone moved, but then the group filed out of the range and down the hall.

Schaefer looked straight ahead as he walked; most of the others looked at Schaefer. Wilcox glared at him with outright hatred; the others' expressions ranged from mild curiosity to open hostility.

Philips tried to hide his own unhappiness behind an angry frown. Lynch had done his best, but without supervision it hadn't been enough. These men were good fighters, but still undisciplined, with no real sense of who they were, what

their job was. Schaefer had picked up on it immediately, pulling that stunt with the target—the men
weren't focused on their enemy, they were focused
on themselves.

That was bad—but there wasn't time to do anything about it.

He led the group into a briefing room and gestured for Schaefer to join him up front while the
others took seats on a few of the dozen folding
chairs. A man wearing captain's bars was standing
at the front, hands clasped behind his back;
Schaefer ignored him and lounged comfortably
against the blackboard, facing the men.

Philips stood between Schaefer and the captain
and announced, "All right, now listen up!"

Schaefer didn't see any change in the seated
audience, but Philips seemed satisfied and continued, "This is Detective Schaefer, NYPD. He'll be
going with us on the mission. He was directly
involved in the New York incident, and he has firsthand knowledge of these creatures. He also speaks
fluent Russian, which means we don't need to
worry about sending along some half-assed translator or teaching a phrase book to any of *you* apes."

"Jesus, you're bound for Siberia and you didn't
teach any of 'em Russian?" Schaefer asked.

Philips turned and glowered at him. "You said it
yourself, Schaefer—it's *cold* in Russia, and those
things like it hot. We've got Lassen there who
knows Arabic, Wilcox speaks good Spanish, Dobbs
has some Swahili—we thought that would probably
cover it, and we couldn't teach them every damn
language on Earth!"

Schaefer nodded. "Fair enough, General."

Philips turned back to the others. "Detective

Schaefer's got an attitude, but hell, so do the rest of you. Take it from me, he knows what he's doing, so damn it, *listen* to him if he tells you something about these creatures. Have all of you got that?"

No one answered, but Philips didn't allow himself to notice. He turned and barked, "Captain Lynch—I want Schaefer combat-briefed on all our equipment and ready to go by 0600 hours. Is that clear?"

"Crystal, sir," Lynch replied smartly.

"Good. Carry on." Philips took a final look around, smiled, and then marched out of the room.

"Lassen, you're with me," Lynch called. "The rest of you, pack up—you heard the general, 0600."

The men rose and scattered; a moment later only Schaefer, Lynch, and Lassen remained. Lynch waited a few seconds, then leaned over close to Schaefer. He grimaced, producing what Schaefer thought might have been intended as a conspiratorial smile.

"Look, Schaefer," he said, "this squad's been training as a team for six months. We don't need some second-rate gumshoe telling us our jobs. The general wants you along, you come along, and maybe we'll use you as a translator if we need one, but otherwise, you just stay safely out of the way and everything'll be fine, okay?"

Schaefer stared coldly at him.

"You're a civilian," Lynch said, trying to explain himself. "You aren't being paid to risk your neck."

"I'm a cop," Schaefer replied. "You think I'm not paid to risk my neck?"

"Yeah, well," Lynch said, "so I phrased it badly. Siberia's still outside your jurisdiction, okay?"

Schaefer stared at him for a second longer,

then said, "You know, I've always heard that it's up to the officers to set the tone for the whole unit. Maybe that's why your men are all assholes."

It was Lynch's turn to stare angrily, fighting to keep control of his temper. Finally he wheeled away and shouted, "Lassen! The general wants this man briefed; brief him, already!"

"This way, sir," Lassen said quietly, pointing at a side table that held a variety of equipment cases.

Schaefer ambled over and watched as Lassen opened case after case and lifted out various items.

"Type 19D Ranger-wear snowsuit," Lassen said, holding up a shiny light-brown jumpsuit. "Thin and practical, with none of the standard bulk to inhibit movement. Tested to fifty below zero."

Schaefer crossed his arms over his chest.

"The suit is warmed by high-pressure, thermally charged fluid pumped through the fabric by an electrical unit worn on the belt," Lassen explained.

"Cute," Schaefer said. "Does it come with matching pumps and a purse? And if it's meant for the snow, why the hell isn't it *white*?"

Lassen ignored the questions and set the body-suit aside. He picked up an automatic rifle.

"M-16S modified ice-killer," he said. "Nice piece of work—you won't find one of these at your local sell 'n' shoot! The barrel and firing mechanism have been crafted out of special alloy steel, perfect for cold-weather firing—again, down to fifty below. It's a . . ."

He stopped in midsentence; he'd lost his audience. Schaefer had turned away.

"Hey!" Lassen called. "Where the hell do you think *you're* going?"

"Toys 'R' Us," Schaefer answered. "They have a better selection of toys." He turned at the doorway.

"Listen, I don't blame *you,* Lassen," Schaefer said, "but you've been brainwashed by this high-tech crap. You and the others think this stuff makes you superior to those things, ready to handle anything they throw at you. You're wrong; you don't know them, don't know what they're like. You've heard the stories, but deep down you don't *believe* them, you still think you're the toughest thing going, with your American know-how and guts and your fancy equipment." He shook his head.

"That's not how it is," he said. "When it comes right down to it, it's going to be *you* against walking death—just you. And when it gets to that point, all the fancy knickknacks in the world won't mean shit, and how tough you *think* you are won't matter. What matters is whether you're ready to do *anything* to take 'em down. I killed one of them once, Lassen, and you know how I did it?"

Lassen shook his head.

"With a big pointed stick," Schaefer told him. "I had guns and lots of other toys, and so did it, but it was a wooden stake through its heart that punched out its lights once and for all." He waved an arm at all the cases. "This crap won't matter. You'll see. It'll probably just make you overconfident and get you all killed."

"No, I . . ." Lassen began.

Schaefer didn't stay to hear what the soldier had been going to say; he marched out, intent on getting a hot meal and a little sleep before they shipped him off to the arctic.

17

Rasche sat at the breakfast table, reading the newspaper. The front-page headline was about the American ambassador to the U.N. publicly calling the Russian ambassador a liar and insisting that there were nukes being moved around illicitly in the arctic, but Rasche was more interested in the funnies—"For Better or For Worse" was his favorite.

He sipped coffee and looked up at the clock: 7:20. It would be three hours later in New York—the middle of the morning.

He lowered the paper. "Shaef never called back, did he?" he asked.

"No," Shari said. She was standing at the sink, rinsing the kids' breakfast dishes.

"That's not like him," Rasche said.

He'd tried calling Schaefer three or four times the night before and hadn't gotten an answer.

He'd left a message on the machine at Schaefer's apartment.

"Maybe he's on a stakeout,".Shari suggested. "If he is, he could be gone for days." She didn't mention all the times Rasche had been gone for days on stakeouts, or that there hadn't been any since they had moved to Oregon.

"Maybe," Rasche admitted. He smiled at Shari to show he wasn't worried, that everything was fine and that he was happy to be out here in Bluecreek. Then the smile vanished. "What the hell," he said, "I'll give him another try." He tossed the paper aside and reached for the wall phone. He knew Schaefer's office number by heart.

Someone picked up on the fifth ring, and Rasche started to relax—but then he realized that the voice on the other end wasn't Schaefer's.

"Detective Schaefer's office, Officer Weston speaking," the voice said.

"Weston?" Rasche frowned. "This is Rasche—is Shaef around?"

"No, he . . ." Weston began. Then he recognized the name. "Rasche? My God, you haven't *heard*?"

"Heard what?"

Shari looked up at the sudden change in the tone of her husband's voice.

"Schaefer's gone," Weston explained. "His whole squad was wasted in a drug sting that went bad—we still don't know what the hell went down, but we wound up with a van full of dead cops, three dead perps, a shitload of questions, and no Schaefer. Rawlings and Horshowski and a couple of techs bought the farm on this one."

"What about Schaefer?" Rasche demanded.

"What do you mean, 'no Schaefer'?" The possibility that Schaefer might have been included in the vanful of dead cops simply didn't occur to Rasche. Schaefer couldn't have died that way; it wasn't his style.

"Schaef's disappeared," Weston said. "Gone without a trace. One reason I'm on his phone is in case someone calls with a lead."

"Schaefer doesn't just *vanish*," Rasche said.

"He took off to Central America that time without telling anyone here," Weston countered.

"Yeah, but he told *me*," Rasche replied. "Look, check around his desk, will you? Appointment book, calendar, maybe he left some kind of note."

"Jeez, Rasche, I don't . . ." Weston didn't finish the sentence; Rasche could hear, very faintly, the rustling of paper as Weston poked around on Schaefer's desk.

"There's some stuff about the sting," Weston said at last, "and a note here on top with no explanation, just a couple of connected names . . ."

"What names?" Rasche asked. He'd been Schaefer's partner a long time; he thought he might recognize names that had never made it into any official records.

"Philips and Smithers," Weston said.

That first name struck Rasche like a thunderbolt. "Philips?" he said. *"Philips?"*

"Yeah, Philips, one *L*," Weston said. "Does that mean anything to you?"

Rasche hung up the phone without answering.

In New York Weston called "Hello?" into the mouthpiece a few times before he gave up and did the same.

Rasche was staring at the wall.

"Honey?" Shari asked. "What is it?"

"Schaef," Rasche replied.

"What about him?" she asked, putting down the last cereal bowl. "Is he okay?"

"He's missing."

"Oh," she said quietly, staring at him.

"I have to go, Shari," Rasche said.

"But if he's missing, how will you know where to go?" Shari protested.

"It's more than that," Rasche said. "It's not just that he's missing . . ." He stopped, unsure how to explain.

Schaefer was his friend, and more than just a friend; he was Rasche's partner, and that held true even if they weren't working together anymore. Schaefer was someone who'd always been there for Rasche whenever he needed him, no matter what, and Rasche had tried to do the same, to always be there when Schaefer needed him.

And if General Philips had turned up again, then Schaefer damn well might need Rasche's help.

If Philips was involved, then two things were certain—Schaefer was in trouble, and it had something to do with those *things*, those murderous monsters from outer space that had been haunting Rasche's nightmares for the past six months. Those were Philips's special province.

Schaefer being in trouble was nothing new; Schaefer lived and breathed trouble, and was a match for just about anything he ran into.

If there was anything on Earth that Schaefer wasn't a match for, though, it was those damned alien creatures—and General Philips.

"I have to go to New York," Rasche said.

"But how . . ." Shari stared at him. "I mean . . ."

"I *have* to," Rasche said simply.

Shari sighed. She'd lived with Rasche long enough to know not to argue. Usually he was a good husband, a thoughtful man, a loving father—but sometimes something would come along that made him suddenly push all that aside, and when that happened there wasn't any point in argument. His sense of duty, of responsibility, was stronger than anything she could say—and that sense of responsibility was part of what made him the man she loved.

"If you're sure," she said.

Rasche pulled on his coat. "Call the mayor for me, would you? Tell him it's a family emergency," he said. "Tell him whatever it takes. I'll be back as soon as I can." He headed for the garage.

Shari watched him go.

"I hope so," she said quietly.

18

The plane was a modified B-2 "Stealth" bomber—modified to carry paratroops rather than bombs.

It hadn't been modified enough to be comfortable, though—the seats were small and hard, the air was dry and cold, and there wasn't anything to drink but water and fruit juice. Wilcox and Lassen had complained about that for most of the last few hours, making the same stupid wisecracks over and over before they finally ran out of steam and shut up.

Schaefer didn't care whether the seats were comfortable or not; the only thing that had been bothering him had been Wilcox and Lassen bitching about it, so he couldn't get some sleep. Now that they had stopped, he had been enjoying the silence, up until Philips emerged from the forward hatch and said, "Well, that's it—we've crossed over into Russian airspace, and the pilot's taking us down low and slow for the drop. ETA at the dropsite is three minutes."

Schaefer stretched and stood up. "You sound pretty damn nonchalant about it," he remarked. "I thought we spent all those billions on defense because we were worried about stuff like Russian radar."

Philips snorted. "They can't even make a good copying machine, and you think we can't beat their radar net? This plane's part of what we spent those billions on, and we got our money's worth."

"You *think* we got our money's worth," Schaefer corrected him. "We won't know for sure until we see whether they shoot it down."

Philips ignored him and gestured to Captain Lynch.

Lynch got to his feet. "All right, you crybabies," he said to Wilcox and the others, "time to earn some of that exorbitant salary we've been paying you. Make your final equipment check and let's boogie." He tripped the switch and the hatch slid open.

Wind howled; nothing but gray darkness showed through the opening, though. Schaefer stepped up closer.

"Looks like a long drop," Lynch said. "Getting nervous, cop?"

Schaefer smiled a tight little smile. "Yeah," he said. "I forgot to set my VCR to record this week's *Melrose Place*. Maybe you'll let me watch yours when we get back."

Lynch glared at him for a moment, then turned away in disgust. "All right, boys," he said. "Do it!"

One by one, the seven men leapt from the

plane—first the four enlisted men, then Schaefer, then Lynch, and finally Philips.

Frigid air screamed up around Schaefer; his goggles protected his eyes, and his high-tech snow-suit protected his body, but the rest of his face stung fiercely, then went numb as he plummeted through space. He jerked at the handle on his chest.

Schaefer's chute opened just the way it was supposed to when he pulled the cord, blossoming into a big off-white rectangle above his head and jerking him suddenly upward, turning his down-ward plunge into a gentle glide—but the cold didn't go away. He grimaced, then tugged experimentally on the lines, and discovered that yes, it steered exactly as it should. So far, so good.

He looked down, trying to pick out a good landing spot, but all he could see was blank gray-ness. At first he thought his goggles had fogged up, but he could still see the other men and their para-chutes clearly; there wasn't anything wrong with his vision, there just wasn't anything to see in the frozen wasteland below.

Well, one patch of snow was as good as another, he thought. He adjusted his lines slightly to keep from drifting too far away from the rest of the team, then just waited for his feet to touch down.

As he descended, he looked around at the others. Philips had really come all this way with them, which surprised Schaefer; the general had to be in his sixties, which was pretty damn old to be jumping out of airplanes over enemy territory or hunting alien monsters.

Philips had guts, anyway.

Schaefer looked down again. The ground was

coming up surprisingly fast. His feet were mere yards above the surface, and Schaefer concentrated on turning his controlled fall into a run, getting out from under his chute before it collapsed onto the ice.

Then he was down on one knee in a puff of powder, the chute spread out behind him. He stood up, dropped the harness, and began reeling the whole thing in. He could tell that the chute was scraping up several pounds of snow, but he didn't worry about it.

The others were landing around him; because of his size, Schaefer had been the first to strike ground. Captain Lynch came down less than fifteen feet from where Schaefer stood.

Lynch threw Schaefer a glance, then looked around for the others.

He spotted one of them helping another up.

"Lassen!" he called. "What happened to Wilcox?"

"I think he landed on his head," Lassen shouted back.

"Guess he didn't want to injure something important," Schaefer said.

Lassen whirled and charged toward the detective, fists clenched. "We're through taking shit from you, Schaefer!"

Lynch grabbed Lassen, restraining him.

Schaefer didn't move. He said, "That's funny— I figured you were up for a lot more yet."

"All right, that's enough!" Philips shouted from atop a snowbank. "We've got a job to do here!"

Lassen calmed enough that Lynch released him; the whole party turned to face Philips.

"There's an oil pipeline that runs just west of

here, the Assyma Pipeline," he said. "Whatever it
was we spotted landed right near it, north of here.
There's a pumping station just two klicks from
here, with a small garrison, some workmen, and
maybe a couple of geologists stationed there—that's
the closest thing to civilization anywhere in the
area. We'll take a look there, see what the Russians
have been up to—if they've been doing anything
with our visitors, they'll have been working out of
that station, because it's all they've got. Keep your
mouths shut and your eyes open, and move it!"

Philips turned and began marching, leading
them toward the pumping station. No one bothered
to say anything as they followed.

For one thing, Schaefer thought, it was too
damn cold to talk. The spiffy electric underwear
really worked, and from the neck down he was as
toasty warm as if he were home in bed, but the suit
didn't cover his hands or feet or head, and his
gloves and boots were plain old heavy-duty winter
wear, with nothing particularly fancy or high tech
about them. He wore a thick woolen hood over his
head, with a strapped-on helmet and his goggles on
top of that, but most of his face was still bare,
exposed to the Siberian wind, and it wasn't much
better down here than it had been a mile up.

It was like having his face stuck in a deep
freeze. His body was warm, but his face was already
just about frozen. His skin was dry and hard, the
sweat and oil whipped away by the wind; when he
opened his mouth it was like gulping dry ice,
burning cold searing his tongue and throat. His eyebrows felt brittle; his nostrils felt scorched.

Odd, how intense cold burned like fire, he
thought.

He wondered how the hell Philips could find his way through this frigid gloom. The night wasn't totally dark; a faint gray glow seemed to pervade everything, reflecting back and forth between the clouds and the snow, though Schaefer had no idea where it came from. Still, everything Schaefer could see looked alike, an endless rolling expanse of ice and snow; how did Philips know exactly where they'd landed or which way the pipeline lay?

Schaefer supposed the general had his compass and some Boy Scout tricks. He seemed pretty confident.

And he had good reason to be confident, Schaefer saw a few minutes later when the radio tower of the pumping station came into view.

Without a word, the soldiers spread out into scouting formation, the men on either end watching for Russian patrols or sentries, all of them moving forward in a stealthy crouch. Schaefer didn't bother—there wasn't any place to hide out here. If they were spotted, they were spotted.

They weren't spotted, though, so far as Schaefer could see. They crested the final ridge and got a good long look at the pumping station.

Gray blocky buildings stood half-buried in the drifting snow, arranged around the central line of the pipeline. All were dark; no lights shone anywhere. Nothing moved.

The place looked dead.

Of course, in the middle of a Siberian winter Schaefer didn't exactly expect to see anyone playing volleyball or sunbathing on the roof, but this place had that indefinable something, that special air that marked abandoned, empty buildings.

"Check out the door, sir," Lassen said, pointing.

Lynch and Philips both lifted pairs of binoculars and looked where Lassen indicated; Schaefer squinted.

He frowned and started marching down the slope, his M-16 ready in his hands.

"Hey, Schaefer!" Wilcox shouted. "Where the hell do you think you're going?"

"Down to take a good look at that door," Schaefer shouted back.

"He's right," Philips said, sliding his binoculars back in their case on his belt. "Come on." Together, the seven Americans moved cautiously down the slope and up to the ruined east door.

Schaefer didn't hurry; it was Lassen who reached the empty doorway first. "I'd knock, man," he said, "but I don't think anybody's home."

Schaefer didn't respond; he'd turned aside to look at something, at a spot of color in this dreary gray and white landscape.

A drainpipe emerged from the base of a wall beneath the pipeline itself. The frozen puddle beneath the drain was dark red—the color of dried blood.

Or in this case, Schaefer thought, frozen blood.

"Schaefer, over here," Philips called.

Schaefer turned and joined the others at the door.

Jagged strips and fragments of steel lay on the snow; only the hinges were still attached to the frame. Schaefer looked at those hinges, at the way they were twisted out of shape, and at the rough edges of the scattered pieces.

"This was cut with a blade," he said. "It's steel, though—you don't chop through that with a pocketknife. And the way these hinges are bent, whatever punched through here went from the outside in." He glanced at the bloody drainpipe. "They've been here," he said. "I can smell it."

"Lynch, get some light in here," Philips said. "We'll take a look inside."

Lynch stepped forward with a high-powered flashlight. Cautiously the party inched into the corridor.

This took them out of the wind, but Schaefer noticed that inside the building didn't really seem much warmer than outside. The heat was off. Whatever might be the case elsewhere in the complex, this one building was dead and deserted—you didn't stay in an unheated building in weather like this.

The power was off, too—flipping light switches didn't do anything.

Lynch shone the light around, and almost immediately they spotted the blood on the wall and the floor—it would have been hard to miss, really, there was so much of it. They glanced uneasily at each other, but no one said anything; what was there to say?

"Down that way," Schaefer said, pointing to a side tunnel.

Lynch glanced at Philips for confirmation; the general nodded, and Lynch led the way around the corner, into the side passage.

"Gennaro, you wait here," Philips ordered one man, pointing at the corner. "You watch our rear."

Gennaro nodded and took up a position at the T of the intersection; he stood and watched as his companions marched on down the corridor they had chosen.

The six men emerged into the maintenance area, and Lynch shone the light around—then stopped, pointing the beam at a drying puddle of something reddish-brown. Slowly he swung the light upward.

"Oh, my God," he said.

Schaefer frowned. "Looks as if those bastards found some time to play," he said.

Lynch moved the light along the row of corpses. To the men below it seemed to go on forever— three, five, eight . . .

Twelve dead bodies hung there—twelve *human* bodies, and to one side, two dead dogs. Crooked lines of something sparkled here and there on their sides, and hung from their heads and dangling fingertips, giving them a surreal appearance—icicles of frozen blood and sweat.

"Hsst!" Gennaro called.

Schaefer whirled; the others, fascinated by the grisly sight overhead, were slower to react.

Gennaro was in the corridor, pointing back toward the demolished external door.

"Something's moving out there!" he whispered. "I heard engines."

"Damn," Philips said. He glanced around, clearly trying to decide who to station where.

"We need to stay together, General," Schaefer said. "If it's those things, they're experts at picking off sentries or stragglers."

Philips nodded. "Come on then, all of you," he said, leading the party back up the passage.

A moment later they were in the outer corridor, grouped along the walls; Schaefer peered out into the dim grayness of the outside world.

"I don't see anything," he said.

"I'm *sure*," Gennaro said. "Over that way." He pointed toward the pipeline.

"Come on," Philips said.

Together, the party moved back out into the wind and cold, inching along the building's exterior wall in the direction Gennaro had indicated.

A sharp crack sounded, and then the singing whine of a ricochet; a puff of powdered concrete sprinkled down over Schaefer's modified M-16.

"Drop your weapons immediately, all of you!" someone shouted in heavily accented, high-pitched English. "You're under arrest!"

Schaefer turned and saw the line of soldiers crouching at the top of the slope, rifles trained on the Americans. The Russians were used to winter conditions; they had been able to move into position undetected, and they now had the Americans trapped against a blank wall, completely unsheltered and vulnerable. And there was no telling how many of them there were; they could have an entire division behind that little ridge.

Schaefer put down his weapon, slowly and gently. At least, he thought, these were human enemies.

They might have a common foe.

19

The lieutenant who approached the Americans with an AK-100 at the ready was small, even in the bulky Russian Army greatcoat, but it wasn't until she lifted her snow goggles that Schaefer realized he was facing a woman.

"You are under arrest," she repeated.

"I don't think that's a good idea," Schaefer said in Russian.

"But I do," the Russian lieutenant said, switching to her native tongue. "You speak Russian. I'm impressed. But whatever language you use, you're still trespassing. American soldiers in full gear, here in the Motherland, tearing up our installations? It won't do."

"We didn't tear up anything," Schaefer replied.

The lieutenant jerked her head at the door.

"You didn't tear up that door? What did you use, a grenade?"

"We didn't do that," Schaefer insisted. "We found it like that. Listen, your countrymen in there are all dead. We'll *all* be dead if we don't cooperate."

"Dead?" The lieutenant's voice caught for a moment; then she continued, "If you are telling the truth, and my friends are all dead, I'll kill *you* last." She shoved the AK-100 in Schaefer's face.

He backed off a step.

"Look for yourself," he said.

The lieutenant glared up at him for a moment, then said, "We will." She shifted her grip so that she held the assault rifle with one hand while she beckoned with the other. "Steshin!" she called. "Take a look in there!"

The man she called Steshin ran up and past her, past the cornered Americans, and through the ruined door into the pumping station. Schaefer could hear the sudden heavy thudding of his boots as the soldier's feet hit concrete floor instead of snow; the sound faded gradually as he advanced into the darkness of the corridors.

"Along the tunnel to the right!" Schaefer called after him in Russian.

"The lights don't work, Lieutenant," Steshin shouted back. "I see blood on the floor."

"Lynch," Schaefer said in English, "give them your flashlight."

Lynch demanded, "Why should I?"

The lieutenant swung her AK-100 to point at Lynch. "Because you will very regrettably be shot while attempting to escape if you do not give Sergeant Yashin that light," she said in clear but accented English. "We have lights in the vehicles, but yours is closer."

Lynch glowered, but handed over his hand lamp. The sergeant who accepted it followed Steshin into the station, and Schaefer could hear two sets of footsteps moving off into the building's interior.

For a long moment the Americans and their captors simply stood, waiting, while the cold soaked into their faces. Schaefer wondered whether those heavy woolen greatcoats the Russians wore kept out the arctic chill as well as the fancy plastic suits—probably not, he thought, but that might not be a bad thing. The contrast between his warm body and his frozen face was not pleasant.

Then one set of footsteps returned—uneven footsteps. Schaefer turned to see Steshin stagger out of the doorway, his face almost as white as the snowy ground.

"Lieutenant," Steshin said, "they're all dead, as he said. And worse. They're hanging like butchered sheep. Blood everywhere."

The lieutenant glanced from Schaefer to Steshin and back, obviously torn; then she ordered, "Guard them carefully. Shoot anyone who reaches for a weapon or takes a single step. I'm going to see."

"Don't move," Schaefer translated for the other Americans. "She just told them to blow our heads off if anyone moves." He put his own hands on his head, just to be safe.

The lieutenant nodded an acknowledgment, then lowered her weapon and strode to the door.

Steshin followed as Lieutenant Ligacheva marched down the east corridor and turned right into the passage to the central maintenance area; the route was dark except for the faint glow of the American's torch ahead and the arctic sky behind, but she knew every centimeter of the pumping station.

She found Sergeant Yashin standing in the doorway to the maintenance area, AK-100 aimed into empty darkness; the light was on the floor at his feet, pointed upward at an angle, up toward the pipeline.

She followed the beam of light and saw the corpses hanging from the girders, brown icicles of frozen blood glittering.

"I saw spent cartridges on the floor," Yashin reported. "No other sign of whoever did this."

"Shaporin," Ligacheva said, recognizing a face under its coating of ice and gore. "And Leskov, Vesnin . . ."

"All of them, Lieutenant. Twelve workers on the crew, twelve corpses. Even Salnikov's dogs."

Ligacheva stared up at them.

She remembered when she had first arrived at Assyma the previous summer. She remembered how both the soldiers and the workers had made fun of her, the only woman at the station; how most of them, sooner or later, had tried to talk her into bed—even the married ones, whose wives were somewhere back in Moscow or St. Petersburg. She had refused their advances and resigned herself to a life of lonely isolation—but it hadn't happened. Her rebuffs were accepted gracefully; her silence in the face of derision was silently acknowledged as a sign of strength. The abuse had faded away.

In the brief Siberian summer the major form of recreation had been soccer games between the soldiers and the workers, played in the muddy open area south of the station. She had played, perversely, on the side of the workers, as an officer could not be expected to take orders from an enlisted man even if he were team captain, and as a woman she was not thought a good enough player to claim the role of captain herself. When she'd demonstrated that she could hold her own on the soccer field, she had been accepted by most of the workers as a worthy companion. And with time, she became more than a companion; some of these workers had been her *friends*.

She tried to remember the smiling, sweaty faces she had seen then, in the slanting orange sunlight after the games. She tried to hold those images in her mind, to not let them be replaced by the frozen horrors trapped in the cold light of the American lamp.

"Steshin," she called. "Take two of the men to the furnace room—it's directly across there." She pointed. "See if you can restore heat to the complex."

Steshin saluted and headed for the door.

"Filthy Americans," Yashin growled. "They slaughtered these oil workers like cattle!"

"These men were slaughtered," Ligacheva agreed, "but not by the Americans. Why would the Americans hack them apart? Why would they hang them up there in plain sight? Do those look like bullet wounds? And why are there no American corpses?" She stooped, picked up the light, and shone it across the floor, picking out a blood-spattered AK-74. "Our men were armed and fired many rounds—why were no Americans harmed?" She shook her head. "Something else did this. Go out there, bring everyone inside, start searching the complex for any sign of who or what might have done this. Bring the big American to me; put the others in the workers' barracks under guard, but bring the big one here. I want to talk to him before whatever did this decides to come back."

She did not mention anything about monsters, about the creature that had butchered her squad out there on the ice—Yashin would not have believed her. She knew, though, that that thing had come here.

Had it come looking for *her*, perhaps?

"The *Americans* did this, Lieutenant!" Yashin insisted. "Barbarians!"

"I don't believe it, Yashin," she said flatly, in a tone that brooked no argument.

Yashin glowered at her, frustrated—she was the officer; he couldn't defy her openly. Still, he had another objection to her orders. "Then if the Americans did *not* do it, how do you know that whatever is responsible is not still here, elsewhere in the complex?"

"I don't," Ligacheva replied. "That's why I want it searched. Now, go get the men in here and bring me the American!"

Yashin grumbled, but he went.

Not long after, Schaefer and Ligacheva stood side by side in the maintenance area, looking up at the corpses. The other Americans were being led past, under guard, on their way to captivity in the workers' quarters.

"I wondered how long it would take you to figure out that we weren't responsible for these Christmas decorations," he said in Russian. "Now maybe you'll listen to reason."

"Perhaps," Ligacheva said as she began to amble across toward the boiler room. Schaefer followed. "Perhaps you know who *did* kill these men?"

"Monsters," Schaefer said seriously. "Boogeymen from outer space."

"You expect me to believe that?"

"No," Schaefer admitted without hesitation. "But I hope you'll admit that you don't have a better explanation, and you'll play along until I can prove it to you."

"Then perhaps I have a surprise for you, American," Ligacheva said. "Perhaps I *do* believe in your monsters from the stars. Perhaps I know more about them than you think."

"And maybe you don't," Schaefer said. "What you *think* you know can get you killed. These things mean *business,* sweetheart."

"Yes, I'm sure they do," Ligacheva retorted. "Thank God the brave Americans have come to save us, with their fancy guns and gaudy suits!"

Schaefer grimaced.

"And of course, the Americans have only come to *help,*" Ligacheva went on. "Your intentions surely couldn't be less than honorable! You flew here secretly and without permission only to save time, I am certain."

Before Schaefer could compose a reply—he spoke Russian fluently, but not as quickly as English—the two of them were interrupted by a thump, a whir, and then a low rumble from the far side of the pipeline. Overhead the lightbulbs flickered dim orange for a moment, then brightened.

"It would seem Steshin has restored power," Ligacheva remarked. "Let us hope heat will follow." They had crossed the maintenance area under the pipeline; now she knocked on the door and called out, "Steshin, will we have heat now?"

"Not immediately, Lieutenant," Steshin called back apologetically. "Someone ripped out pieces here and there—flow control valves for the oil pumps, capacitors . . . it makes no sense what they took. Nothing seems to have been smashed deliberately, but parts were taken away." He opened the door, allowing Ligacheva and Schaefer to peer into the boiler room—Schaefer noticed that a certain warmth still lingered here, despite the ruined external door and the fierce cold outside.

He also noticed spent cartridges scattered on the floor and sprays of dried blood on the floor and door frame. Someone had put up a fight here—not that it had done any good.

"The missing parts aren't on the floor?" Ligacheva asked, looking around at the clutter of tools and plumbing that Steshin had strewn about in the course of his repairs.

"No, Lieutenant, they're gone, gone without a trace," Steshin told her. "I had to patch the emergency generator around the main board directly into the lighting circuits to get us any power. To get oil to flow to the boiler I would have to rig replacements for those missing valves, and I don't know how—I'm a soldier, not a mechanic."

"Well, do what you can," Ligacheva said.

"Lieutenant!" someone called from the far side of the maintenance area. Ligacheva turned to see a figure gesturing wildly from one of the corridors. "Back there! Down the other tunnel! He's . . . he's . . ."

Ligacheva saw the direction the soldier was pointing, and a sudden realization struck her. She dashed forward far enough to see past the pipeline and looked up at the corpses, more hideous than ever in the restored light.

"Twelve of them," she said, counting quickly. "Twelve workers, Galyshev and his men—but there was Sobchak!"

"Who?" Schaefer asked.

"Come on," Ligacheva told him, striding down the passage toward the scientific station.

Schaefer hesitated, glanced around at the Russian soldiers standing on all sides with weapons held ready, and then followed the lieutenant through corridors that gleamed white with hoarfrost in the unsteady glow of the bare lightbulbs. Icicles hung in glittering lines from the overhead pipes; Schaefer had to smash them away with one gloved hand to avoid ducking his head, and his progress was plainly audible as ice rattled to the floor and crunched underfoot.

The final tunnel opened into a bare concrete room, the floor slick with a thin layer of black ice. A soldier was standing at an open door on the far side of the room—a mere kid, Schaefer thought, cold and scared despite the machine gun he held and the uniform he wore. He might be eighteen, Schaefer supposed, but he didn't look a day over sixteen.

"Lieutenant," the soldier said, his voice unsteady but relieved at the appearance of a superior. "He was lying there, he wouldn't let me touch him—he wouldn't even tell me his name . . ."

"Sobchak," Ligacheva said. "Oh, God. His name is Sobchak." She pushed past the soldier and stared into the room, expecting a scene of blood and devastation, expecting to see that the monster had attacked Sobchak.

Nothing was out of place; nothing had been disturbed. Many of the metal surfaces were white with frost, instead of their normal gray, but the equipment was all in place. Most of the meters and screens were dark—apparently someone had shut many of the devices down, or the cold had ruined them, or perhaps the restored power Steshin had provided was not sufficient to power everything. Certainly, the lighting throughout the station seemed dimmer than usual.

And the air in this laboratory was far, far colder than the rest of the station, almost as cold as outside. Ligacheva frowned.

"Where . . ."

The soldier pointed, and Ligacheva saw Sobchak, lying on his back on the floor, his hands and feet bare—and horribly discolored, red and purple and black.

Severe frostbite. Ligacheva had seen frostbite a few times before, though never a case this bad, and she recognized it instantly.

"So tired of white," Sobchak muttered, holding one of his ruined hands above his face. His voice was scratchy and thin—the cold had damaged something, Ligacheva was sure, his lungs or his throat. "So tired of the cold and the white," he said. "Isn't it pretty?" He waved his arm, and his dead hand flopped limply. "See? Isn't it pretty?"

Ligacheva hurried to the scientist's side and knelt. "Sobchak, it's me—Ligacheva," she said. "What happened? You've got to tell us what happened."

Sobchak turned his head to look at her, struggling to refocus his eyes. She saw that his left ear was black with frostbite, too. "Ligacheva?" he said. "Yes, yes, yes. I remember you."

"Sobchak, what happened?"

"I hid," Sobchak replied. "I was scared—I heard the screams, and the door was locked, and I didn't dare . . . My boots were outside, but I . . . and the cold, the heat stopped and I still didn't dare . . ."

"Yes, I see," Ligacheva said. "I see completely, but you're safe now. We'll get you to a doctor."

She knew it was probably far too late for that; Sobchak was almost certainly dying, and even if he lived he would lose both his hands and feet—which might be a fate worse than death for the little scientist.

"They left," he said. "I charted them with the equipment, the seismographs . . . but I was still scared. And I didn't know how to fix the heat anyway."

"I understand, Sobchak," Ligacheva said.

"I drew a map," Sobchak said.

"Here," Schaefer said, spotting the one piece of paper that had not been touched by the frost that had condensed from the once-moist air. He picked it up and turned it to catch the light.

"You," Ligacheva said, pointing at the soldier at the door. "I want a medical crew up here on the double!"

The kid saluted and hurried away. Schaefer watched him go, then said, "Our friends seem to be based in or near a canyon or ravine about eighteen or twenty kilometers from the station." He added, "That's assuming your pal here was better at drawing maps than he was at keeping his socks on, anyway."

Ligacheva jerked upright, then turned to glare

at Schaefer. She rose to her feet and snatched the map out of his hands without looking at it; she stood staring angrily up at Schaefer. The top of her head didn't quite reach his chin, but that didn't seem to matter.

"A man's dying and you talk as if it's some petty inconvenience," she said. "What kind of a man *are* you, to make a joke of this?"

Schaefer stared down at her for a moment without speaking; then a voice from the doorway interrupted.

"Lieutenant, on the radio—an urgent message from Moscow. General Ponomarenko!" The voice was Sergeant Yashin's.

"Coming," Ligacheva answered without turning. She stared at Schaefer for a second more, then pivoted on her heel and strode away.

Schaefer silently watched her go, then nodded once to himself.

"Tough chick there," he said in English. "Asks good questions."

20

Sergeant Yashin stood by impassively, listening as Lieutenant Ligacheva argued with her superior. The two of them were alone in the cramped little radio room, the lieutenant operating the equipment while Yashin watched the door.

"General, you don't understand," Ligacheva said desperately. "Yes, we have Sobchak's map, we know where their base is—their ship, or whatever it is. But we can't attack it yet—it's impossible!"

"Nothing is impossible," Ponomarenko replied.

"We've just arrived, sir," Ligacheva insisted. "We haven't even secured the Assyma complex, haven't even cut down the bodies, let alone done any reconnaissance. We don't know anything about what's out there . . ."

"You do not *need* to know," Ponomarenko interrupted. "Soldiers are often faced with the unknown, my dear. The arrival of these Americans necessitates an immediate attack—we *must* have firsthand information on whatever is out there before the site is further compromised. We have no way to be certain you have captured *all* the Americans."

"General, if we go out there now, it may well be a repeat of what happened to my previous squad. I cannot accept the responsibility . . ."

Ponomarenko cut her off. "Is that your final word, Lieutenant?"

"I . . ." Ligacheva hesitated, then straightened up. "Yes, sir," she said. "That's my final word."

"In that case, Lieutenant," Ponomarenko said, "you may remain at the pumping station with the prisoners." Ligacheva began to relax, then snapped to attention as the general continued, "Sergeant Yashin will lead the attack."

"Sergeant Yashin?" Ligacheva turned and watched as a wolfish grin spread over Yashin's face.

"Yes. Is he there?"

"Yes, he's here, sir," Ligacheva said slowly.

"You heard your orders, Sergeant?" Ponomarenko asked.

"Yes, *sir*," Yashin replied happily.

"That will be all, then, Lieutenant."

"Yes, sir," Ligacheva said. She put down the microphone and stared at Yashin.

"You planned this, didn't you?" she demanded.

"I thought an opportunity might arise," Yashin said calmly, hands clasped behind his back. "I let the general know that he could put his faith in me."

"Just in case he had any doubt of it," Ligacheva said bitterly.

"Indeed," Yashin said, rocking gently on his

heels. "*You* may be content with your present rank and status, Lieutenant, but I am not—I have hopes for advancement. One can scarcely live on a sergeant's pay these days, and they do not give commissioned rank to men who simply do as they're told and show no initiative."

"Your initiative may get you killed out there," Ligacheva pointed out.

"I do not think it will," Yashin sneered. "I am no mere woman, frightened of the cold and the dark and caught unawares. I will confront our enemy boldly, as you could not. While you're here tending the Americans, let *real* soldiers take the field, Lieutenant—we'll show you how it *should* be done, so we can finish this matter and return home to our warm beds, our women, and our drink."

Ligacheva stared at her sergeant for a long moment.

Maybe, she thought, Yashin was right, even if he was a traitorous bastard. Maybe he and the other men were more than a match for their enemy. Maybe they would capture whatever was out in that canyon. She hoped so.

She didn't believe it, though.

She believed that Yashin would lead them all to their deaths.

But there was nothing she could do about it. He had his orders, and his opinions—he wouldn't listen to anything she had to say.

So she didn't bother saying it. She turned away without another word and went to find the American, Schaefer—and the bottle of vodka that Galyshev had always kept put away in the cabinet in his office.

21

Rasche had caught a cab from Kennedy to Police Plaza. He wasn't on the force anymore, but he still had friends, and he was still in law enforcement, and law officers cooperated with each other; he had known that Police Plaza was the place to start.

He talked to Weston and to half a dozen other old friends and acquaintances and got the gory details of the bad bust that had left Baby, her two flunkies, and four good cops dead. On the basis of ballistics, Forensics had tagged one of the victims, Arturo Velasquez, with killing the four cops, but had no solid leads on who had taken out Arturo and his friends—none of the bullets matched any of Schaefer's known personal arsenal or any of the weapons found at the scene.

Baby and Reggie had each taken a 9mm slug through the head, execution style; no 9mm guns were involved elsewhere in the incident, however. Schaefer owned several handguns, but none of them were 9mm.

No one mentioned the fact that most federal agents carried 9mm pistols.

The crime scene had been messy, but nothing like the slaughterhouses those creatures had left behind the previous summer; this carnage was clearly all the work of human beings, not monsters from outer space.

The guys who had been working in the comics shop had been interviewed—Rasche couldn't keep straight who was who in the statements, since they all seemed to be named John, but it didn't matter, since their stories matched. They reported seeing men in dark suits out front, but had no useful descriptions beyond that—they'd dove for cover as soon as the shooting started, and they had stayed down, out of the field of fire, until all the shooting had stopped.

And no one had any idea what had become of Schaefer in all this chaos. When the shooting had finally stopped he was simply gone, and the men in the dark suits were gone with him. The lab said that none of the bloodstains at the scene were Schaefer's; all of them matched neatly with one or another of the known dead. That meant that Schaefer had probably still been alive when he vanished.

Rasche was pleased to hear that—pleased, but not surprised. He wasn't entirely sure it was *possible* to kill Schaefer.

He was a bit less pleased that none of the bloodstains or fibers provided any leads on the men in suits. "Feds," Rasche muttered at the mention of the dark suits. Everyone knew that federal agents generally favored dark suits. "Philips," Rasche said.

As soon as Weston had mentioned the name Philips, Rasche had known that somehow Schaefer was involved with those *things* again, those sadistic predators from outer space.

Who the hell was Smithers, though? Rasche had never heard of any fed named Smithers.

Smithers was his *lead*, that was who Smithers was.

Rasche didn't have legal access to the NYPD computers anymore, but his friends did, and they were glad to "demonstrate" the system for a visiting sheriff. Military records brought up 212 entries under "Smithers" for personnel on active duty; Rasche was able to eliminate most of them at a glance.

When he got to one of them he stopped looking. The match was good enough that Rasche didn't see the need to look any further.

Smithers, Leonard E., age thirty-four, U.S. Army colonel, involved in CIA operations dating back to the Reagan administration, present assignment classified. Commanding officer, General Eustace Philips.

Philips. Philips and Smithers. That had to be the right one.

Smithers had an office address in midtown listed—and, Rasche decided, it was time for a certain Oregon sheriff to pay that office a visit.

Getting a cab was easy—that was one thing he had missed about New York. If you wanted a cab in Bluecreek you phoned Stan's Taxi and waited forty minutes. You didn't just step off the curb and wave. And you could just forget about buses or subways.

On the other hand, in Bluecreek he didn't have to listen to Greek cabdrivers talk about how everyone blamed the Serbs, when it was the Albanians who caused all the trouble. It was a relief to escape onto the sidewalk and into the nondescript office tower.

The building had a military guard in dress uniform in the lobby; Rasche flashed his badge. "Rasche, Bluecreek sheriff's department—I'm here on police business. Colonel Smithers, please."

"Yes, sir," the guard said, hauling out a register bound in dirty blue vinyl. "Room 3710. Please sign in, stating the reason for this visit."

Rasche smiled and signed in; for his reason he scrawled, "To kick some ass."

The guard either didn't read it or didn't care; he didn't say a word as Rasche stamped down the corridor and boarded an elevator.

Rasche didn't like seeing the military involved in Schaefer's disappearance. Schaefer's brother Dutch had disappeared without a trace years before, when he'd been on some secret rescue mission and had run up against the alien hunters; he'd lost his squad but come out of the whole business alive, and *then* he'd vanished. The last thing anyone admitted seeing of him was when he'd gone in to be debriefed, for the umpteenth time, by the military.

Maybe the U.S. Army had taken a hint from the old Argentines or Salvadorans and had disappeared Dutch. And maybe now they'd done the same thing to Schaefer.

Or *whatever* had happened to Dutch, maybe it had happened to Schaefer.

Except that Rasche wasn't about to *let* it, despite what the U.S. Army might want. Yeah, he was all in favor of a strong military, but there were limits, and he intended to point this out to Colonel Smithers.

Room 3710 was a small office located halfway down a long, drab corridor. The windowless, off-white door was ajar, and Rasche pushed it open.

A big, short-haired man in a dark suit was sitting on the corner of the desk, holding the phone. ". . . got a tee-off time at six," he was saying as Rasche entered. "We can . . ." Then he spotted Rasche and stopped in midsentence.

"Colonel Smithers?" Rasche asked.

"I'll call you back," Smithers said into the receiver. He hung up the phone, then turned to Rasche and demanded, "Who the hell are you?"

"Concerned taxpayer," Rasche said. "Got a minute?"

"Hell, no." He started to say more, but Rasche cut him off.

"Think you could find one? It's important."

"Listen, mister, whoever you are," Smithers said, "I'm not a recruiter or a P.R. officer. Was there something you wanted?"

"As a matter of fact, yes," Rasche said. "My name's Rasche, Colonel. Maybe you can guess what I'm after."

"No, I . . ." Smithers began. Then he stopped, and his tone changed abruptly from annoyance to uncertainty. "Did you say 'Rasche'? *Detective* Rasche?"

"It's Sheriff Rasche now, actually," Rasche said, shrugging diffidently. "I don't want any trouble, Colonel. I was just wondering whether you could tell me where my old partner has got to. Detective Schaefer."

"Get out of here, Rasche," Smithers said, getting up off the desk. "You don't want to be involved."

"Oh, now, don't be too . . ." Rasche began as Smithers approached him.

Then Smithers reached to grab Rasche's shoulder and shove him out of the office, and Rasche made his move.

In all his years on the NYPD, Rasche had always left the tough-guy stuff to his partner as much as he could. One reason he had liked being partnered with Schaefer was that Schaefer was so *good* at the tough-guy stuff. Schaef was about six and a half feet tall, classic buzz-cut Aryan with big broad shoulders and visible layers of muscle; he looked like he'd been carved out of stone by a sculptor with a body-building fetish. Schaefer didn't have to hit people much because one look at him convinced most folks that they weren't going to win if it came to blows—and they were right, too, because Schaefer was at least as tough as he looked.

Intimidating people just by looks saved everyone a lot of trouble, and Schaefer did it better than anyone else Rasche had ever met.

Rasche, though . . . Rasche was about average height, with a potbelly wider than his shoulders, with bony arms and a Captain Kangaroo mustache. He looked about as intimidating as one of those inflatable clowns with the weighted bases that kids used to punch.

That had its uses, too. He couldn't intimidate anyone with his looks, but he could catch them off guard. In fact, he'd made it his specialty. Tough guys *always* underestimated the fat old cop when he smiled and shrugged and talked in that polite, vague way he'd worked so hard to perfect.

Smithers was just one more. He reached out for Rasche's shoulder and made no attempt at all to guard himself. Rasche's hands, locked together, came up hard and fast and took Smithers in the side of the head with most of Rasche's two hundred pounds behind them.

Smithers staggered sideways, caught off-balance, but he didn't go down until Rasche kneed him in the groin and then rammed both fists down on the back of his head.

Rasche shook his head as he closed and locked the door; was this the best the feds could do? Smithers had recognized Rasche's name, so he'd probably read up on some of what Schaefer and Rasche had done together. Had he thought that it was all Schaefer, with Rasche just going along for the ride? The hoods on the street had always thought so, which was just the way Schaefer and Rasche had wanted it, but the feds ought to know better.

It was almost enough to hurt his feelings, he thought as he hauled the moaning, semiconscious Smithers into the chair behind the desk. How the hell did Smithers think Rasche had ever made detective in the first place and picked up his several commendations?

Five minutes later Smithers was fully conscious again and tied securely into his chair with the cords from his phones and computers. Rasche smiled across the desk at him.

"Darn it, Colonel," he said, "I thought this could be a friendly chat. After all, all I want to know is what happened to my friend."

Smithers stared at him.

"You'll go to prison for this, Rasche," he said. "Assaulting an on-duty federal officer is a felony . . ."

Rasche cut him off. "Yup," he said, nodding. "It sure is a felony, and a serious one. But are you really going to want to go into court and testify in front of a judge and jury and your superiors about how an over-the-hill small-town sheriff caught you off guard and trussed you up like a Thanksgiving turkey?" He smiled again, and that walrus mustache bristled; his eyes narrowed, and he really didn't look a thing like Captain Kangaroo anymore.

"Besides," he added, "I have a hunch that your boss, my old friend General Philips, really wouldn't care for the bright lights of a civilian trial, since if it came to that I'd be doing my best to turn it into the biggest media circus since O. J. Simpson."

Smithers frowned uncertainly.

"Anyway," Rasche continued, "that's all beside the point." He reached under his jacket. "I want to know what happened to Detective Schaefer, and I want to know *now*." He drew the .38 Police Special out slowly, and then, moving with careful grace, brought it out to arm's length and aimed it directly between Smithers's eyes.

"That gun doesn't scare me, Rasche," Smithers said scornfully. "I know you're a cop; you wouldn't *dare* pull that trigger."

Rasche shook his head. "Yeah, I'm a cop," he said. "And cops don't go around shooting people who don't answer questions—at least, *good* cops don't." He pulled the gun back for a moment and looked at it contemplatively. "So you know I'm a cop, Colonel, but are you ready to gamble your life that I'm a *good* cop? I've had a pretty bad time lately, you know; I left the force here in New York after that mess on Third Avenue, but that didn't really end it. It's still bothering me. I almost strangled my dentist the other day." He aimed the gun again. "I'm not sure just what I'm capable of anymore. I've gotta say, though, that I'm pretty sure I'm not *that* good a cop anymore. Remember that I'm just full of surprises, Colonel—I took you down a few minutes ago, didn't I?"

Smithers cleared his throat but didn't speak.

Rasche leaned forward across the desk, bringing the .38's muzzle to just an inch or two from Smithers's face. "I've heard about you military guys who get assigned to the CIA for their dirty tricks," he said conversationally. "Special training, psychological counseling—you think you can handle just about anything, right? Well, I didn't have all that. What I had instead was a dozen years on the streets, where I learned all about what people will and won't do. Maybe you learned some of the same things I did in those fancy classes of yours." He leaned closer, and Smithers pulled as far away from the gun as his bonds would allow. "I want you to look into my eyes, Colonel," Rasche said, "and I want you to use that special training to see inside me, to understand exactly what I'm feeling right now and what I'm capable of. If you read my file, I want you to think over everything it said in there—I got some commendations, yeah, I got promoted, but I also got in my share of trouble, didn't I? Insubordination, brutality . . . you think about that."

Rasche's voice had gradually dropped from a normal tone to a whispered growl, and Smithers had begun to sweat. "Think about all the things that make life *good*, Colonel," Rasche murmured. "Oreos, moonlit nights, the laughter of friends over a few beers, the soft touch of a woman's hand. You think about all that *very carefully*, Colonel, and then I want you to ask yourself a question." Rasche paused and adjusted his grip on the .38 so that there was no chance it would jerk out of line if he pulled the trigger.

"Ask yourself," he said through gritted teeth. "Do you really want to die today?"

And Smithers started talking.

22

iberia!" Rasche said as he charged out onto the street. "Christ almighty, *Siberia?*" He looked both ways for a cab, didn't see any—but when he briefly considered taking the subway the newsstand beside the subway entrance caught his eye. A stack of papers displayed the headline RUSSIANS DENY U.S. MISSILE CLAIMS.

He'd looked through a Chicago newspaper on the flight east and caught the usual snatches of news from radios and CNN and the like—it was hard to completely miss a major story in a news-saturated American city. Now the pieces fell into place.

"Shit," Rasche said. "Siberia!"

There weren't any illegal nukes being moved around, no Russian nationalists or separatists or terrorists threatening the U.S., he realized. That was the cover story, fabricated by someone in

Washington to hide another monster hunt—and the Russians weren't willing to counter it with the truth because *they* wanted to get their paws on the aliens' high-tech goodies, too. That stuff could put their economy back on track, make them a real world power again without having to actually teach their people how to run businesses.

Half a dozen cabs finally appeared, a platoon of bright yellow Chevys charging up Sixth Avenue, vying with each other for position—they still seemed to hunt in packs, Rasche saw, the same as when he'd lived in the Big Apple. He flagged one down; it swooped in toward the curb, spraying Rasche's pant legs with dirty slush.

"Where to?" the driver asked as Rasche climbed in.

Rasche hesitated.

The feds weren't going to be cooperative— Smithers had made that plain. They'd shipped Schaefer off to Siberia to help out their team of monster-hunters, but they weren't interested in Rasche, or he'd have heard from them already.

And it was a little late to volunteer, in any case—the mission had gone in. So he'd need to get to Siberia without any help from the feds.

In theory, he could go back to Kennedy and book a flight on Aeroflot to whatever commercial air-field was closest to the Yamal Peninsula, wherever the hell the Yamal Peninsula was, but what would he do from there? He didn't speak Russian, didn't know a thing about getting around there, didn't know exactly where the alien ship was.

If he wanted to find this place where the alien ship had landed, he'd need a guide, someone who knew his way around, knew what was going on.

And he had an idea how to find one.

"The U.N.," he said.

The cabbie didn't ask any questions or start talking about Serbians; he just swung east at the next corner and headed downtown.

Rasche sat in the back of the cab, watching the familiar streets and buildings stream by, thinking over what he was getting into.

From what he'd heard on CNN and seen in the headlines, Pentagon spokesmen had been making threats, talking about a preemptive strike. The Russians had been countering with warnings of retaliation for any uninvited intrusion. Commentators talked about the sudden chill in U.S./Russian relations, and how even if this particular problem were cleared up there might be lasting damage. The whole world was closer to World War III than it had been at any time since the Soviet Union collapsed.

And all along, Rasche thought, the people in power, the people making threats and counter-threats, surely knew that there weren't any misplaced nukes involved.

He used to wonder sometimes what had made Schaefer so bitter, what had happened to convince him that the human race was worthless, what had made it so hard for him to feel, to care about anything.

At that particular moment, Rasche thought he knew.

He didn't give a shit about the politics involved in this mess; he was a loyal American, but that didn't mean he had anything against Russians, or that he thought much of General Philips and company. Those clowns weren't fighting for Rasche's idea of freedom, democracy, or America—they were acting out of simple greed, out of a quest for power. They wanted to have the military strength to tell the rest of the world to go to hell, and they didn't care how they got it.

Not that the Russians were much better. Somehow Rasche doubted that Moscow was going to share the alien technology with the peoples of the world, should they happen to acquire it, and if someone like that loon Zhirinovsky ever got elected president over there it could be bad news—but that wasn't Rasche's problem. The generals could smack each other around until doomsday for all he cared.

What he cared about was Schaefer. He was dealing with the world on a smaller, more personal scale than the generals and bureaucrats. He'd always figured that if everyone did that, if everyone minded his own affairs and lived up to his own responsibilities without getting any big ideas, the world would be a better place.

Rasche didn't know much of anything about politics, but he did know that he wasn't going to let *anyone*—not the feds, not the Russians, not the aliens—mess with his friends or family while he sat by and did nothing.

He paid the cabbie and marched into the U.N. Secretariat Building.

"Where do I find the Russian ambassador?" he demanded at the lobby information desk.

The guard started to give him the standard brush-off, but Rasche pulled out his badge and went into his "serious problem" speech.

Ten minutes later he was pounding his fist on a receptionist's desk, demanding immediate admittance to the inner office.

"You can't barge in on the ambassador without an appointment," she protested.

"Just tell Boris, or Ivan, or whatever the hell his name is, that I know about that thing in Siberia," Rasche told her. "Tell him that, and he'll see me. It's on the Yamal Peninsula at a place called Assyma—I know all about it. I know about the American team that's gone in . . ."

"Sir, I don't know what you're talking about," the receptionist said.

"But I do," a deep voice said.

Rasche and the receptionist turned to look at the gray-haired man standing in the inner doorway.

"I heard the commotion," the gray-haired man said.

Rasche had expected that; that had been the whole point of being loud and obnoxious in the first place.

"I'm sorry, Mr. Ambassador," the receptionist said. "He was very insistent."

"It's all right, my dear," the gray-haired man said soothingly. "Send the policeman in."

Rasche smiled.

"Oh, and please, Sheriff," the ambassador said as he ushered Rasche inside, "my name is not Boris or Ivan. I am Grigori Komarinets."

23

Ligacheva slid the brimming shot glass across the table to Schaefer.

"Here, American," she said bitterly. "A toast to Yashin's success."

Schaefer stared expressionlessly at the drink. The vodka was Stolichnaya, of course, and the glass was reasonably clean, but he didn't pick it up right away.

Ligacheva lifted her own glass and contemplated it. "So eager to engage the enemy, my Sergeant Yashin. So eager to taste first blood," she said.

"They're all going to die," Schaefer said flatly. "All those men."

Ligacheva paused, her glass of vodka in hand, and stared at him.

"Yashin is acting just like those things," Schaefer told her. "He lives for the fight, the thrill, the blood." Schaefer picked up his drink and swallowed it. "Hell, maybe we *all* do." He thumped the empty glass down on the table. "The thing is, they're *better* at it than we are. So Yashin and the rest are all going to die."

Ligacheva lowered her drink and set it gently on the table, still untouched. "I thought you Americans were the world's great optimists," she said. "You talk of freedom and peace and color television, and you go about your lives happily certain that someday you'll all be rich . . ." She shook her head and stared at Schaefer. "So what happened to *you*?" she asked.

Schaefer reached for the bottle. "I got a look at the American dream," he said. "Two-car garage, June Cleaver in the bedroom, one and three-fourths kids—and a Smith & Wesson in the dresser drawer, just in case things don't quite work out." He poured. "Except lately it seems the cars are in the shop, June's on Prozac, the kids are on crack, and the Smith & Wesson's getting plenty of use."

"I don't know this Prozac," Ligacheva said. "And I don't know what you're talking about."

"It doesn't matter," Schaefer said. He bolted the second shot. "Look, you think I don't care what happens to your men—maybe I don't. Maybe I can't care anymore. But that's nothing. What matters is that *nobody* cares. The people who put us here sure don't give a shit. We're just numbers to them, an allotment, another piece of equipment; we're low tech and easy to maintain."

Ligacheva shook her head and gulped her own first drink. "That can't be true," she said. "Some don't care, maybe—there are always bad ones."

"*Nobody* cares," Schaefer insisted. "Except those things out there. That's why they're going to win—because they *believe* in what they're doing here. Nobody sent them. Nobody ordered them to come. Nobody screwed them out of their jobs, or their freedom, or their lives. They come here because they *want* to, because it's *fun*."

Ligacheva frowned. "You seem to believe you have a special understanding of these creatures. You say these things as if you *know* them."

"Maybe I do," Schaefer said. "I've survived dealing with them once, anyway, which most people don't. I understand enough about them to know there's something wrong about their being *here,* in this place."

"Explain."

"They don't care much for the cold," Schaefer told her. "I should know—the last time we met, the only thing that saved my ass was a half inch of summer rain. They like it hot—so what the hell are they doing *here*? And they come here to hunt, to kill people for fun, to collect our skulls as trophies— well, I don't see a lot of people around here, do you? Besides, if they *were* here to hunt us, if they *really* wanted us dead, we'd have been hanging from the yardarms hours ago, like your friends down the corridor."

"Why are they here, then?" Ligacheva asked. "Why *did* they butcher Galyshev and the others? My squad—they killed them, too, but maybe we were intruding, getting too close to their base. But what did the workers do? You say they hunt for fun, as we hunt animals—all right, where is the sport in such a slaughter? And why ruin our heating system?"

Schaefer shook his head. "Those workers were just in the wrong place at the wrong time, would be my guess," he said. "Whatever they were after, I don't think the aliens were looking for those men. Hell, I don't think those things wanted to be here at all. I think this is a detour, the wrong exit— something went wrong and landed them here, and they don't like this shitty weather any more than *we* do. They're in a bad mood, and your buddies got in the way, that's all."

Ligacheva shuddered.

"They took things," she said. "Pieces from the pumps and the wiring."

"Spare parts," Schaefer said. "Their ship . . . maybe something's broken, and they're trying to fix it." He considered the bottle thoughtfully, and then put it down without pouring a third drink. "Must be like trying to repair a Porsche with whalebone and baling wire," he said in English. He didn't have the Russian vocabulary for it.

"Surely, these things are capable of great ingenuity," Ligacheva said in Russian.

"Surely," Schaefer agreed. "Aren't we all?"

As Ligacheva and Schaefer spoke in the pumping station's common room, the other Americans sat dejectedly in the military barracks.

"This is *embarrassing,*" Dobbs said. "The Russkies took us down before we could get off a shot!"

"I want to know what happened to that lousy cop," Wilcox said. "We're freezing our asses off in here while he's kissing up to that butch lieutenant . . ."

"Shut up, Wilcox," Lynch said. "All of you shut up."

"Why?" Wilcox demanded.

"So we can plan how we're going to get out of here and what we're going to do once we're out,"

Philips told him. "Did anyone see where they put our gear?"

"That storeroom across the hall," Lynch said. "But, sir, I don't see how we're going to get out of here."

"Our orders were to secure the alien ship," Philips said, "and we sure as hell can't do that from in here, now can we?" He reached down and pulled a flattened cylinder from his boot—the Russians had taken their packs and had patted them down, but the search hadn't been very thorough. "So we grab our equipment, we secure the station, and then we head out for that ship. Now, give me a hand with those mattresses . . ."

A few moments later the guard at the barracks door heard shouting and banging. He turned, startled.

He had had English in school, of course— everyone did. He hadn't used it in years, though, and he had never actually spoken English to anyone outside a classroom. He struggled to make out words through the locked door.

One voice seemed to be doing all the shouting. "Hey!" the American called. "You out there! You speak English? Ever seen a Super Bowl? You watch *X-Files*? What's the capital of Sacramento?"

The guard could not follow that. He struggled to remember the words he wanted.

"Slow," he shouted back. "You talk slow, please!"

"The door!" the American shouted.

The guard frowned. He knew *that* word. It was almost like the Russian. "Door" meant *dvyer*. He unslung his AK-100 and stepped closer to the door. "What, door?" he asked.

"It's got *termites,* bozo!" the American shouted.

The guard had no idea what the American was talking about, or what "termites bozo" might be. He stepped up and put a hand on the door.

It seemed solid enough. It was cold to the touch—*extremely* cold—so the crazy American wasn't worried about a fire.

"What, door?" he repeated.

"C-4 termites!" the American said.

The blast smashed the door upward and outward—the lower hinge was torn from the frame instantly, since the C-4 charge had been almost at floor level, and the lock gave as well, but the upper hinge held at first, so that the upper two thirds of the door pivoted up like a gigantic pinball flipper and smashed the guard off his feet. The explosion reduced the bottom third of the door to bits and drove four-inch splinters into the guard's legs, belly, and groin.

Inside the barracks the blast was absorbed by the stacked mattresses that had been piled on top of the little surprise package from Philips's boot. The sound was still startling, almost deafening.

"Come on," Philips barked, leading the way over the resulting heap of cotton stuffing, broken wood, and blood.

24

Ligacheva and Schaefer both jerked upright in their seats at the sound of the explosion. "The barracks!" Ligacheva said. She called to the guard at the door, "Galan, stay here—be ready for anything. I'll take the American with me."

She rose, beckoned to Schaefer, and headed briskly down the passage.

Schaefer followed, noticing that Ligacheva was not bothering to keep a close eye on him. He wasn't sure whether to take that as a compliment or an insult; she seemed to trust him, but when it came right down to it, she had no business doing so.

If he turned aside and lost himself somewhere in the mostly empty complex, she might never find him—but she wasn't the enemy, despite what Lynch and company might think, despite what she herself might think.

Besides, he wanted to know what the hell had blown up. He could always slip away later.

The two of them headed down the station's central corridor at a fast trot, then turned the corner into the passage to the workers' barracks.

There they both stopped dead. There was no need to go any farther to see what had happened, where the explosion had been. The Russian guard lay sprawled on the floor, staring sightlessly at the ceiling, and the smell of explosive and charred wood filled the passage.

No Americans were in sight.

"It would appear that your friends have escaped," Ligacheva said. "As has my guard, in a different sense."

"They're soldiers, Lieutenant," Schaefer said. "That's their job."

She didn't answer right away. Instead, she started to step forward for a closer look at the debris.

As she did, she heard the scrape of boots on concrete. Before she could take a second step, an American appeared in the doorway of the nearby storeroom and pointed an M-16 at her—the American captain, Lynch. Ligacheva started, and realized that her hands were empty, that she held no weapon. She had left her AK-100 back in the common room.

Annoyed with herself and seeing no alternative, she raised her hands in surrender. The American captain smiled.

"They do their job better than I do mine, it would seem," Ligacheva said.

"For the moment," Schaefer agreed.

"Hey, cop," Lynch said, "speak English."

"I wasn't talking to you," Schaefer said.

"Fine, then. Talk if you like. I don't know what you two are jawing about, but you know what? Right now I don't much care. We've got our thermal suits and our cold-weather guns and enough ammo to take down Rhode Island, so I don't guess it makes any difference what you're saying." He gestured with the M-16. "Give me a hand with some of this stuff, and we'll go join the others."

Schaefer stepped up to the storeroom door; Lynch tossed him a heavy backpack, which he caught one-handed.

"So Philips is running the show again?" Schaefer asked, slinging the pack on his shoulder.

"The general's talking to the brass, and until he's done with that, *I'm* in charge," Lynch said. He hefted another pack. "You know, Schaefer, somehow, as long as we've got this stuff, I don't think the Russkies will give us any more trouble. Yessir, there's a new sheriff in town around here."

"Your playsuits and your weapons," Ligacheva said in Russian. "Ah, you have your precious toys back, and now you are *invincible!*"

Lynch glowered uncomprehendingly at her. "Shut up and move," he barked, pointing eastward down the main corridor. "Schaefer, what's she saying?"

"She's admiring your aftershave, Lynch," Schaefer said. "Shit, who *cares* what she's saying? The Russians aren't the problem, Lynch! Can't you get that straight?" He started striding down the corridor. "Where's Philips? He'll tell you . . ."

"I told you, the general's put me in charge while he sets up our satellite uplink," Lynch interrupted.

"So tell this Russkie lieutenant to have her boys surrender ASAP, or we'll spam 'em into dog food."

Schaefer grimaced. Lynch had apparently forgotten that the lieutenant spoke good English. Somehow, given what Schaefer knew of Lynch, this did not surprise him.

"What does he say?" Ligacheva asked in Russian. "His accent is too thick, and I don't know all those words."

"This asshole wants me to tell you that if you and your men don't give up, we're *all* dead." They were approaching the side passage to the pipeline maintenance area—apparently that was where Lynch was directing them.

Ligacheva didn't reply, and Schaefer glanced at her; somehow, he didn't believe that she was quite as resigned to capture as she appeared.

"Got any ideas?" Schaefer asked.

"Just one," Ligacheva said in Russian. "Fuck him," she concluded in English. She grabbed Schaefer by the shoulder and yanked him in front of Lynch's M-16, then started running for the smashed east door.

Schaefer was caught off guard and allowed himself to be shoved between Lynch and Ligacheva. He glanced back at Lynch, then at the fleeing Russian woman, and in an instant he decided he preferred Ligacheva, and to hell with nationalities; he'd rather join her out in the snow than hang around with Lynch and the other assholes Philips had brought along. He began running himself, following Ligacheva.

Behind them Lynch hesitated, unsure whether Schaefer was chasing the Russian or fleeing with her; in either case the cop was between himself and the woman, and he didn't think the general would be pleased if someone shot his civilian advisor in the back.

The two of them ran out into the wind and snow while Lynch was still debating with himself, and then the opportunity was gone.

The bitter wind tore at Schaefer's face as he ran; his cheeks went numb almost instantly, while from the neck down he remained eerily warm.

"Jesus, it's cold," he muttered as they charged up the slope, and the moisture in his breath froze into ice on his upper lip almost as soon as the words left his mouth. His short-cropped hair provided almost no insulation, and he didn't have his helmet—his scalp tingled with cold.

"The temperature has been falling," Ligacheva said.

"Christ, it wasn't cold enough? Wasn't it about sixty below?"

"Sixty . . . ?" Ligacheva glanced back at him. "Do you mean Celsius?"

"Fahrenheit," Schaefer said as they topped the ridge. "Not that it matters much. Where are we going, anyway?"

"To join Sergeant Yashin, perhaps?" Ligacheva suggested. "He, at least, fights the right foe. Sixty below zero in Fahrenheit would be minus fifty or so, wouldn't it? That sounds close. But it's colder now, much colder."

Schaefer did not want to think about the fact that he was exposing bare skin to something significantly more than sixty degrees below zero. That was colder than any place in North America ever got, and this Russian seemed to be taking it right in stride. "So where's Yashin?" he asked.

Ligacheva pointed to the tracks in the snow, then ahead, to the northeast.

"Halt!" someone called in Russian.

Ligacheva stopped dead instantly; Schaefer stumbled another few steps, then dropped flat to the snow at the crack of a rifle shot.

He got cautiously to his feet to find the lieutenant facing a young Russian soldier with a smoking AK-100.

"Kazakov," Ligacheva demanded, "what are you doing out here?"

"The sergeant left me on guard," the soldier explained. "Why are you here, Lieutenant?"

"The Americans have escaped and captured the station," Ligacheva replied.

Kazakov blinked at her, and Schaefer noticed that his lashes and eyebrows were white with frost. "What should we do?" he asked unsteadily.

"You have a radio?"

"Wait a minute . . ." Schaefer began, but before he could say any more, Kazakov swung the AK-100 to point at the American's chest.

"Don't shoot him," Ligacheva said. "He's our translator, and the only one of the Americans with any sense. Call Sergeant Yashin."

"Yes, sir." Kazakov lowered his weapon and reached for the radio in his shoulder pack.

Schaefer got slowly back up on his own feet and picked up his dropped pack, realizing as he did that he didn't know just what Lynch had given him to carry, or whether it was worth hauling along.

This didn't seem to be the time and place to check it out, however, with the two Russians watching him. Instead he stood and waited as

Kazakov managed to make intermittent contact with Yashin's expedition.

Schaefer couldn't make out the conversation over the howling of the wind, and didn't seriously try; instead he watched the ridgetop, waiting to see if Lynch or one of the others might be coming after them.

"They're on their way back," Kazakov reported a moment later.

"So now what?" Schaefer demanded. "You trying to work these idiots up into a pitched battle?"

Ligacheva stared up at him calmly. "You said they would all die if they went to face the monsters unprepared," she said. "I am trying to prevent that. Perhaps we can all work together and find some way to defeat these things."

"The best thing we can do is just leave them alone and let them go," Schaefer said. "They don't want to be here, and either they're going to leave as soon as they can, or the cold's going to kill them."

"And you want them to simply depart?"

Schaefer smiled a vicious, tight smile. "No, I want the bastards dead," he answered. "I never liked them much in the first place, and I saw what they did to your people back there. Nobody should do that to good men and get away with it. I don't give a shit about their technology, though, and I don't think we've got what it takes to take them all down, and I don't want to lose more good men trying. I'm hoping the cold will get them all."

"And if it does?"

"Then you and Philips can fight about who gets to study the shipwreck."

"I would prefer that we not fight at all—except,

perhaps, against those creatures. Do you really think there is nothing we can do?"

"Oh, we can fight," Schaefer said. "If they come after us I'll fight them. But I'm not going to walk into any traps if I . . ." He paused, listening.

He could hear the rumble of engines over the wind.

"Yashin," Ligacheva said. "Come on." She turned and led the way up to the ridgetop.

Schaefer followed.

Lynch and the others had taken up defensive positions around the east door, he saw—they had learned from their earlier mistake not to be caught out in the open. Schaefer spotted Wilcox crouched behind a huge pipe; Dobbs had dug into a hollow in the ice beneath a vent, while Lassen stood at the southeast corner of the building, and Lynch himself crouched in the doorway. Gennaro was climbing a service ladder to a post on the station's roof.

Philips was nowhere in sight.

"What do they think they're doing?" Ligacheva asked. "Why are they trying to keep possession of the pumping station in the first place?"

"It's their turf now," Schaefer said in English. "They're challenging Yashin to a pissing contest, that's what they're doing."

" 'Pissing contest'?"

Schaefer could not remember a Russian equivalent. "Never mind," he said. "Look."

He pointed as a Russian APV ground into sight over a snowdrift and headed for the station, its headlights throwing spotlights on Lynch and Dobbs. A second vehicle followed close behind.

"That's Sergeant Yashin," Ligacheva said, pointing to a man climbing out of the first vehicle. "He had not gone as far as I thought."

As she spoke, Schaefer heard a noise behind them; he turned to find a third, much smaller vehicle pulling into the shallow valley where Kazakov had been standing guard.

Ligacheva waved to the driver; he was, Schaefer saw, alone in the vehicle.

"I was sent to fetch you, Lieutenant," the driver called. "You and Kazakov."

"Thank you, Maslennikov," Ligacheva replied. "I think we had best wait a moment, however." She turned to look down at the confrontation below.

Just then a single shot sounded, clearly audible despite the wind.

They didn't see who had fired first, but seconds later the air was full of the rattle of automatic weapons fire and the red lines of tracers.

"Shit," Schaefer said as he dropped to his belly to make himself a smaller target.

Ligacheva was right beside him; Kazakov stumbled back off the ridgetop, into the darkness, while Maslennikov stayed in his vehicle.

"So much for international cooperation," Schaefer said. "Looks like we'll kill each other before those alien bastards get the chance."

Ligacheva nodded. "Yashin has been ready for a fight since he arrived, eager to defend the Motherland; your men seem to be happy to oblige him."

Schaefer watched for a few seconds, then squinted. "Do you have binoculars?" he asked Ligacheva.

She turned and called into the gloom, "Kazakov! Field glasses!"

The private scrambled back up the ridge and

handed the lieutenant the glasses, which she passed to Schaefer. He peered through them.

It hadn't been his imagination; where Wilcox had leaned against the pipe something yellow was dripping from his arm. A smear of the stuff was on the pipe, too.

It wasn't blood; Wilcox might be an asshole, but he was human, and in the light from the Russian vehicles there could be no question that that seeping fluid was yellow, not red. Then what . . .

The suits. Schaefer looked down at his own arms in the brown plastic thermal suit. The suits were filled with circulating fluid, and that had to be what that yellow stuff was. Had Wilcox been hit?

He lifted the glasses and watched.

Gennaro, up on the roof, flung himself prone— and yellow goo sprayed up as if he'd belly flopped into custard. The seams along either side of the suit had burst.

Schaefer snatched off one of his gloves and prodded experimentally at his own suit with rapidly freezing bare fingers.

The plastic had gone brittle. The suit hadn't been intended for weather *this* cold, for the strains of warming and cooling, for the stress of battle.

Siberia, Schaefer knew, was the second coldest place on Earth, behind only Antarctica—the North Pole itself, thanks to the Arctic Ocean, wasn't as cold as Siberia in midwinter. Nothing in North America came close; the army could have tested the suits in the worst weather Alaska or Greenland could throw at them and never had any problem, but that didn't mean they'd hold up *here*.

All the seams in Gennaro's suit must have split open when he flopped down like that.

"Shit," Schaefer said as he pulled the glove back on.

And then Gennaro's gun exploded, spraying metal splinters that gouged into his face, barely missing his eyes.

More of the same, Schaefer thought, as he watched Gennaro roll onto his back, clapping his hands over his injured face. Steel goes brittle in extreme cold—that was what had done in the *Titanic,* he'd heard; the cold water of the North Atlantic had turned the metal brittle, so a mere brush with the iceberg had popped rivets in all directions, and the ship had snapped right in two as she went down.

Modern steel was a lot better than the crap they used for hull plates in 1912, and the M-16s were meant for cold weather, sure, but not for anything *this* cold.

"Minus sixty, Celsius," Ligacheva said.

That would, Schaefer realized, be about seventy-five below zero, Fahrenheit. Lassen had said the equipment had been tested to minus fifty degrees.

Not good enough.

Dobbs's gun blew next. After that it wasn't more than five minutes before the Americans, disarmed by the same General Winter that had defeated Napoleon and any number of other would-be conquerors who had dared to invade Mother Russia, threw up their hands in surrender.

"If you keep the weapons warm whenever you aren't actually firing, under your coat or in a vehicle, they're less likely to malfunction," Ligacheva remarked conversationally. "And you must keep them well oiled, of course—oil is a fine insulator.

When the gun feels dry to the touch it isn't safe in weather like this."

"The voice of experience," Schaefer muttered as he watched Yashin and his men round up Lynch and the others. "Too bad Philips spent so much time recruiting me, instead of someone who really knew cold weather." He remarked aloud, "Looks like your sergeant has everything under control."

"Yes," Ligacheva agreed. "Yashin has wanted control all along. Let him have it."

Schaefer looked at her. "Aren't you going to go down there and take charge?"

"No," she said quietly. She turned to Kazakov and called, "You and Maslennikov, go down there and tell Yashin he's done well," she said. "I'll come presently. Leave the vehicle; I'll drive it down."

Kazakov saluted. A moment later he and the driver marched up over the ridgetop, waving and shouting so that they wouldn't be mistaken for an enemy.

"Presently?" Schaefer asked.

"It is a word that means nothing specific," Ligacheva said. "I will return when I'm ready."

"And what are you planning to do now?"

Ligacheva looked him in the eye. "You came here as an advisor on these monsters, but it does not seem to me that either your people or mine have been very interested in taking your advice. *I* am interested, though." She pointed to the vehicle. "I'll use that. You said to leave the creatures alone. Well, that advice I will not take. I am going to find that ship and get a good look at these things that have killed so many of my friends, and if I can, I will destroy them. To destroy them, the more I know, the better, and I *will* destroy them. I would therefore be pleased if you came along as *my* advisor on how best to do that."

Schaefer stared at her for a moment, then nodded. "It's that way, yes?" he said, pointing to the northeast.

"That way," she agreed.

Together, they headed for the waiting vehicle.

25

It would have been conve-
nient, Yashin thought as he and his men herded
the prisoners through the corridors, if at least one
of the Americans could speak Russian. Trying to
communicate in his own miserable, half-forgotten
schoolboy English was a nuisance.

Then he stopped in his tracks, thinking. When
they had captured the Americans before, there had
been that big American who had spoken Russian,
the one the lieutenant had spoken with so freely.

What had happened to him?

For that matter, what had happened to Lieutenant Ligacheva? She should be here trying to
reassert her authority, and she wasn't.

She had spoken to Kazakov and Maslennikov
outside, in the valley beyond the little eastern ridge,
and then . . . then what? Where was she?

"What the devil is keeping the lieutenant?" he demanded of Kazakov.

"I don't know, sir," Kazakov said. "She was just over the ridge, talking to that American . . ."

"An American?" Yashin frowned. The lieutenant still had the big American with her?

What was she up to?

This would not do, Yashin thought. This would not do at all. Lieutenant Ligacheva was no fool. She was a woman, and perhaps in consequence she lacked a man's true fighting spirit or love for the Motherland, but still, she was not stupid. She knew that Yashin was bucking for a promotion at the cost of her own standing, and she would not want to pay that cost. Whatever she was doing out there with the big American would not be in Yashin's own best interests, he was sure—and probably, if it involved that American, would not be in the best interests of Russia, either.

"Kazakov, Kurkin, Afanasiev—you stay with the prisoners. If they try anything, kill them." There were still half a dozen other loyal men somewhere in the station, if the Americans had not killed them; that would be enough. "The rest of you, come with me."

He turned and headed for the vehicles.

"Something tells me this overgrown snow-mobile isn't going to make it," Schaefer muttered to himself.

Ligacheva didn't hear the words, but she didn't need to. She knew what Schaefer had to be saying. The little snow tractor was dying; she wasn't sure whether it was succumbing to the fierce cold, or whether it was simply out of fuel, but the engine was sputtering and banging.

Then it stopped completely.

She tried not to think of the eighteen or twenty kilometers they would have to walk in the unforgiving cold of the arctic night in order to get back to Pumping Station #12, once they were done with whatever they might do here. First they had to survive their investigation of the alien ship.

"Now we walk," she said. "We're almost there—the tractor wouldn't have taken us much farther in any case."

"So we walk," Schaefer agreed. "After all, we wouldn't want our noisy engine to bother anyone, would we?" He grabbed one of the spare blankets from the little vehicle's storage compartment before climbing out into the darkness and wind; he had never entirely trusted the Pentagon's spiffy little electric suits, and after seeing Gennaro's sleeves dribbling yellow gook he wanted something more to protect him from the wind and cold. He wished he still had his helmet, which was probably back in the pumping station's common room, but settled for pulling the blanket over his head like a hood.

It didn't help much; his ears started stinging with cold almost immediately. He ignored that as he stepped forward into the beam of the headlights and took a good look at what lay ahead, and why they would have had to stop the tractor soon in any case.

He was able to walk another fifteen feet or so; then they were standing on the brink of a ravine, a split in the ice fifty yards across and at least twenty yards deep.

Ligacheva studied Sobchak's map as Schaefer looked over the area.

"They're on the other side?" he asked.

"No," Ligacheva said. "Not according to Sobchak's measurements." She pointed. "Down there."

"Perfect," Schaefer growled as he studied the dim expanse of jagged rock and ice, the shadows and cul-de-sacs and natural ambuscades. "Perfect for *them*. If it was my ass on the line and this was my front walk, I'd have this hole booby-trapped with all the ordnance I could find."

Ligacheva nodded. "As would I—and some things are, I fear, universal," she agreed. "So—how do you Americans put it?" She smiled at him, a humorless, toothy smile, and concluded in English, "Watch your step." She turned and started to clamber down over the canyon rim.

"Wait a minute," Schaefer said. He jogged back to the vehicle, then reached inside and pulled out two packs—the one he had been given by Lynch, and one that had been in the vehicle's storage bin. "Might be something useful in these," he said as he ran back up to the rim. He tossed the pack from the little truck to Ligacheva.

She nodded and slung the knapsack on her shoulder before resuming her climb.

Ten minutes later, halfway down the canyon wall, Schaefer's foot slipped on an icy protrusion. The sudden jar was enough to snap his handhold off the wall, so that he slid four or five feet down the slope clutching a chunk of dirty ice before catching himself on a narrow ledge.

He wasn't injured, but the rocks left long white scratches down the front of his snowsuit, and his fingers were blackened with dirt.

They would have reached the bottom of a mere rock wall in half the time, he thought; it was the ice coating every hold and the snow hiding every weakness that made the climb so treacherous and slowed them to a mere crawl.

"And this is the *easy* way?" he said.

"Nothing is easy here, Detective," Ligacheva called from below. "You should know that by now." She laughed and lost her own hold, sliding a few centimeters, just as a sharp crack sounded.

At first Schaefer thought a larger-than-usual chunk of ice had broken somewhere, but then he heard the unmistakable whine of a ricochet and saw the puff of snow where Ligacheva's head had been a few seconds before.

"What—?" Ligacheva turned her head, staring upward to see what was happening.

Standing on the rim of the canyon, fifty meters away, was a man with a rifle—a man in the heavy khaki overcoat of a Russian soldier.

"Yashin?" she said, astonished.

She had known that Sergeant Yashin disliked her, known he was ambitious and saw this mission and her alleged weakness as his great opportunity for promotion, but to attempt to *shoot* his superior officer? It was madness!

But in that case, he was clearly mad. That had not been a warning shot; she looked at the silver bullet scar in the ice above her. That shot had been meant to kill her.

Up on the rim the half-dozen men hung back and watched as Sergeant Yashin took aim again.

"Sergeant, are you *certain* of this?" a soldier asked uneasily.

"Of course I'm certain!" Yashin barked. "She's

a traitor! Why else did she come out here with the American, without any of us, without *telling* us? They must be planning to steal the alien technology and sell it to the Americans! Or since he abandoned *his* companions, maybe to the highest bidder—do you want the Chinese to have it?"

"No . . ."

"Then she and the American must be stopped!" Yashin said, his finger tightening on the trigger. It was a fairly tricky shot; the lieutenant was half-hidden in the uneven, icy wall of the crevasse, and the light was terrible. Still, he knew he had her.

Then something bright red flicked across his vision for an instant. He blinked and glanced down.

Red dots were scanning across his chest, weaving about; then they focused into a neat triangle.

"*Chto eto*?" he asked. "What is this?"

Then white fire blazed, and a sound like thunder echoed from the walls of the canyon.

To the soldiers behind Yashin the light was blinding; they saw the blue-white flash, then a spray of dark red mist as what was left of the sergeant's body was flung backward. Then they stood, blinking, eyes trying to readjust to the gloom of the arctic night.

One of them finally stepped forward to where Yashin's corpse lay smoking on the ice.

His chest had been ripped apart, ribs bare and blackened; no more blood was flowing because the heat of the blast had cauterized the blood vessels. There was no question at all that the sergeant was dead.

"What happened?" someone demanded.

"He's dead," replied the soldier who had first stepped forward.

"How?"

"Ligacheva and the American," someone else replied. "*They* must have killed him!"

"I don't know . . ." said the man looking down at Yashin's corpse.

"Who else could it have been?" the other demanded. He pointed down into the canyon. "Do you see anyone else down there?"

The man in the lead looked down into the ravine and could see no one but Ligacheva and Schaefer, still inching down the rocks—but it was dark down there, and there were dozens of places to hide among the rocks.

"I see no one else," he admitted, "but this— what could they have that would do this?" He gestured at the body.

"Some secret American weapon," another soldier replied. "The Americans love secrets."

For a few seconds the six of them still milled about uncertainly; then Maslennikov took charge and said, "Follow them!"

Meanwhile, Schaefer and Ligacheva had completed their climb down into the darkness of the ravine. With Yashin's shooting and subsequent death as their inspiration they had descended the last few meters a little more quickly than they had planned; Schaefer had dropped his blanket and stooped to retrieve it when he reached bottom. His now-brittle, scratched, and battered electric snow-suit had stopped working, he noticed; the power supply had scraped against something as he slid down the rocks, and wires had torn loose. Even if the current had still been flowing, Schaefer doubted the suit would have lasted much longer; yellow fluid was oozing from a crack on one knee, and yellow drops seeped from the scratches on his chest.

"Looks like Yashin got someone down here angry," he remarked as he wrapped the blanket around his head again. "Probably one of their security guards." In English he added, "Goddamn rent-a-cops can be somethin' when they're pissed."

"Be careful where you step," Ligacheva replied. She had pulled a flashlight from her pack and was sweeping the beam across the ice ahead of them.

"They'll see us!" Schaefer shouted when he spotted the light. "The men up there, I mean—the creatures can probably see in the dark anyway, from what I've seen."

The light stopped on something that glittered, something that wasn't ice.

"It would appear that your 'rent-a-cops' have left us a souvenir," Ligacheva said. "I would not like to step on that, whatever it is."

"Okay, okay," Schaefer admitted, "so maybe the light was a good idea. Now turn it off!"

Ligacheva did—just as a rifle cracked and snow spat up from a bullet impact.

"Jesus!" Schaefer said. "Your boys up there are stubborn! I thought that even if seeing Yashin's head blown off didn't send them running home, they'd take their time about coming after us again." He turned.

The Russians had secured ropes, Schaefer saw, and were lowering themselves down the wall of the crevasse. Judging the speed of the shadowy shapes was difficult, but it appeared to Schaefer that the climb that had taken Ligacheva and himself fifteen minutes would only keep these fellows occupied for about fifteen seconds.

They were obviously a lot more stubborn than he had realized. They weren't turning back or hesitating; instead they were already in active pursuit again.

"Back!" Ligacheva shouted at the descending soldiers, waving frantically. "Go back! It's not safe down here!"

An AK-100 stuttered, and bullets shattered ice at the lieutenant's feet.

"I don't think they're listening," Schaefer said as he swept an arm around Ligacheva and snatched her off her feet. He slung her over one shoulder and ran.

He hadn't forgotten the traps, though; he deliberately chose an indirect, inconvenient route, pushing himself partway up the scatter of debris along the base of the canyon wall, squeezing between outcroppings where those eight-foot hunters from space wouldn't fit. The instant he found something approximating shelter behind a slanting slab of rock and ice he stopped, lowered Ligacheva, and turned to watch.

The first of the Russians stepped off his rope and charged forward—impaling himself almost instantly on a spearhead that seemed to appear from thin air. He gasped once, tottered, and fell forward.

For a moment the spear supported him; then the incredibly sharp spearhead cut through his spine and he slid forward down the shaft.

Blood ran down the shaft ahead of the dying Russian, and he landed facedown in a pool of his own blood, cooling quickly on the ice.

The spear was snatched from his back by a

shadowy, indistinct figure, and the second man down cut loose with his AK-100, spraying bullets at the barely glimpsed spear-wielding killer.

The thing moved so fast it almost seemed to be dodging the bullets as it turned and ran back down the canyon. The Russian charged after it, bellowing.

He never saw the thing he stepped on, never saw the curving metal strips that snapped up out of the snow and drove spikes into his sides and shoulders, trapping him instantly. His AK-100 flew from his grip.

One spike had rammed through his cheek, so that he could not move his head without inflicting further injury; he was caught staring directly ahead. He could not look away as that shadowy figure stopped, turned, and came slowly toward him.

He could have closed his eyes, but he did not—he wanted to see what he faced, what it was that had trapped him.

It wasn't quite so shadowy and indistinct now. The soldier could see that the thing he faced stood two and a half meters tall and was shaped more or less like a man, its wrists and shoulders sheathed in jagged black machinery that looked somehow barbaric, its face covered by a metal mask and ringed by black tendrils.

The spear in its hand was already red with blood.

It raised the spear very slowly as it advanced.

"Gunin!" one of the Russian's companions called.

Gunin couldn't turn his head to see whether help was coming; the spike would tear open his cheek if he tried.

"Shoot it!" someone barked.

"I'd hit Gunin!"

"Shoot it anyway!" the other shouted. "He's probably dead already!"

That was Pushkov's voice—that bastard! Gunin had never liked him. Gunin tried to open his mouth, to shout that he was still alive, but the pain stopped him—the spike was pressing against his jaw muscles.

Someone, Pushkov or someone obeying Pushkov, fired; Gunin felt burning lines of pain as bullets tore through his right sleeve and through his arm, but the pain was not bad, not enough to make him scream—the spikes had already hurt him enough to deaden his sensitivity.

The creature holding the spear seemed to side-step the bullets easily.

Then it jabbed the spear forward, and Gunin no longer worried about spikes or bullets or anything else as the thing cut his heart out with a single quick gesture.

After that, the alien disappeared, blurring into invisibility.

The other Russians never saw what hit them—but even so, it took several long minutes for them all to die.

26

Ligacheva tried to run, tried to leave the narrow gap between icy boulders that Schaefer had squeezed them both into, tried to go help her men. Schaefer grabbed her arm and held her back.

"Let me go!" she said. "Let me go! My God, Schaefer, look at what's happening to them! I have to help my men fight that thing!"

"You can't help," Schaefer told her. "You'd just die like the others. Those things are doing what they do best, and we can't stop them."

Ligacheva tugged uselessly against his grip.

"Besides," Schaefer added, "a few seconds ago 'your men' were trying to kill us."

"They're still my men!" Ligacheva shouted.

Schaefer stared at her for a moment as she realized the futility of struggling.

"Do you have any idea just how stupid that sounds?" he asked her.

She whirled to face him. "Do you have any idea just how *cruel* you sound?" she replied. "Isn't there *anything* you care about?"

Schaefer frowned.

"*I* care about something," she told him. "I care about my men!"

"Yeah, I care about something," Schaefer said. "I care about the fact that when that thing's done with your friends, it'll probably find us. Do you have a knife?"

She blinked up at him. "A knife?"

"Those things are fast enough to dodge bullets, if they see them coming," Schaefer explained. "And even if you hit them, they're damn near bulletproof. Knives, well . . . they can dodge knives, too, if they have a chance, but I don't intend to give this one a chance."

"There's an entrenching tool in my pack," Ligacheva replied. "I hear the Spetznaz use them like axes when they need to."

Schaefer nodded. "That'll do," he said. "Give."

Ligacheva tore open her pack, trying to ignore the high-pitched screams coming from the other side of the sheltering boulder. Schaefer snatched the entrenching tool from her before she could pull it completely out, and an instant later he was gone.

She blinked. Schaefer had seemed to move almost as fast as that *thing*.

He wasn't invisible, though, and the monster usually was; how could he hope to find it? She stared into the darkness, trying to see.

Schaefer didn't worry about finding the creature; he knew where to look. Those creatures didn't just kill and move on; they liked to play with their prey even after it was dead. All he had to do was watch the corpses . . .

There.

Even in the dim arctic gloom he could see the faint rippling in the air above one of the dying Russians. Most people would have missed it entirely, or dismissed it as some sort of optical illusion, but Schaefer knew what to look for, and he had good eyes.

What he did worry about was how to make his attack. The entrenching tool was strong, all in one piece, not like the folding ones American forces used, and one side was sharpened to a razor edge—but the creature's back was mostly bone, and those bones weren't necessarily arranged like human ones. If he got a shot at the thing's belly he'd have a better chance of doing some real damage—but of course, he couldn't sneak up on it from the front.

He wasn't sure he could sneak up on it in any case. His only hope was if it was too busy with its victim to notice his approach.

All the screaming had stopped. Schaefer wondered if any of the Russians were still alive.

The body the thing knelt over flipped over suddenly, and Schaefer didn't think that movement was the Russian's doing—the creature was getting ready to cut out the man's spine for a trophy.

Something flickered blue, and the creature was visible, kneeling over the corpse; Schaefer wasn't sure whether it had turned off its screen deliberately, or if something had given out in the cold. At any rate, this was clearly his chance—or at least the best he was going to get.

"Hey!" Schaefer shouted, charging at the

monster with the entrenching tool raised. "Remember me?"

The alien turned, startled, just as a man would, and Schaefer swung his improvised weapon.

The sharpened edge skidded across the creature's chest, drawing glowing yellow-green blood, but the blade didn't bite deeply.

Schaefer took another swing, backhanded, and reached his free hand out to grab the thing's mask. He'd tried that trick before, last summer in New York, and it had worked pretty well then . . .

The monster was still half-crouched, off-balance, trying to rise. It grabbed at the entrenching tool and caught it, stopping it dead in midswing—but it had caught the tool by the blade, and the razor edge sliced into the palm of the thing's hand. Luminescent yellow-green blood dribbled slowly onto the snow underfoot.

Schaefer grabbed the edge of the creature's mask and twisted, trying to blind it; at the same time he tried to pull the entrenching tool free.

The tool didn't move; it was like pulling at a steel post. The mask, though, shifted awkwardly.

The thing staggered, confused. It pulled the entrenching tool from Schaefer's hand and flung it away, then reached both hands up to straighten its mask, but before it could recover, Schaefer threw his full weight against it. It tripped over a dead Russian's leg and toppled backward into the snow, its mask coming off in Schaefer's hand.

Gas hissed, and the creature roared deafeningly.

Schaefer threw himself on top of the thing's chest, his knees on its arms, pinning it. Then he raised the mask over his head in both hands and brought it slamming down edge first on the monster's face.

"Hell, New York wasn't so bad," Schaefer said as he raised the mask for a second blow and saw yellow-green ooze dribbling from the thing's hideous, multifanged mouth. "At least I could grab a hot dog when you bastards weren't in sight." He swung the mask again. "Siberia, though—Siberia *sucks*. I'm freezing my fucking *ass* off out here!" He drove the yellow-smeared edge of the mask down onto the thing's eyes for his third blow and felt the creature twitch beneath him. "What the hell did you want to come here for, anyway? Go *home,* why don't you?"

The thing roared again, and something whirred.

Schaefer froze, the mask raised for a fourth blow.

"Uh-oh," he said as the black shoulder cannon began to pivot toward him. He flung himself backward, and the blue-white fireball roared up into empty space.

"Go home!" the creature bellowed, in Schaefer's own voice, as the detective scrambled to his feet and the cannon began to home in for a second shot.

Schaefer dove sideways, but the white fire, whatever it was, tore the skin from one side of his scalp.

"Bastard!" Schaefer said as he staggered, trying to keep the blood out of his eyes. One hand flew up to feel the wound and found hair and flesh gone. "You son of a . . . That was a new haircut!"

The alien was on its feet now, and plainly in control of the situation again; the cannon stayed up and ready, but didn't lock on or fire again. Instead, the creature advanced deliberately toward Schaefer.

It was bleeding from a gash across its chest, and

one hand and its mouth were dripping greenish goo—Schaefer was able to see that much, even dazed as he was. At least he had hurt the thing.

In fact, it looked angry. It was so alien Schaefer couldn't be sure, but he thought something about the eyes looked really seriously pissed.

"Come on, stud," he said, struggling to stand upright and meet the thing head-on. "Give us a kiss."

The creature didn't say a thing as it stepped toward him; it just raised its right fist.

With a click, those double blades on the back of its wrist snapped into place.

"You!" someone shouted.

Schaefer blinked away his own blood in time to see Ligacheva leap forward as the creature turned its head. The thing had been so focused on Schaefer it hadn't seen the Russian . . .

Or her weapon. Ligacheva had an AK-100 in her hands, and when the monster turned to face her she thrust the muzzle into its open mouth and fired.

The specifications for the AK-100 say it fires six hundred rounds per minute, but the standard magazine only holds thirty rounds—three seconds at full auto. Standard use is two- or three-shot bursts, to conserve ammunition.

Ligacheva, just then, didn't give a shit about conserving ammunition; she kept the trigger jammed down tight until the full clip was expended.

That was perhaps the longest three seconds of Schaefer's life as Ligacheva emptied the weapon into the monster's face. The creature didn't budge; it stood and took it as glowing yellow blood and shredded yellow flesh and fragments of white, needle-sharp teeth sprayed out the back of its skull.

One clawed hand reached toward the heavy gauntlet on the opposite wrist, as if trying to reach some of the controls on the wristband, then fell limp. The black tube on the left shoulder rose up and began to swivel.

Then, at last, as Ligacheva's finger clicked uselessly on the trigger of an empty weapon, before the shoulder cannon could lock on to its target, the creature tottered and fell, toppling forward onto the lieutenant, knocking her flat on her back in the snow.

The shoulder cannon jerked and fell still.

Schaefer cleared his eyes of blood as best he could and staggered over to where the two of them lay. Ligacheva, trapped beneath the thing, stared up at him with terror-filled brown eyes.

"Is it dead?" she asked unsteadily, her breath little more than a gasp due to the weight on her chest.

Schaefer bent down and heaved the thing off her, rolling it to one side.

"It's not exactly dancing," he said. He sat down abruptly, not caring that the action split the seams on the thighs of his snowsuit, spilling yellow goo a few shades lighter than the stuff smeared all over the dead alien.

At least the stuff from the suit didn't glow in the dark, he thought.

Then he looked over at Ligacheva, who was sitting up now, staring down at her dead foe.

"Nice save," he said. "Thanks."

"Is it over?" she asked. "Was this what killed all my men and the workers at the station?"

Schaefer looked around carefully before answering, peering both ways down the canyon.

"I get the feeling that old Lunchmeat here was just a security guard," he said. "A sentry, keeping an eye on things. If there were more right here we'd probably be dead by now, but I'd bet there are more of them down the road there, just where your scientist buddy's map says the ship is."

Ligacheva got to her feet, brushed glowing slime from the front of her overcoat, and looked down at the dead creature. "If it is as you say," she said, "its friends will not be happy when they learn this one is gone."

Schaefer smiled humorlessly and wiped blood from his face again. "I'd say you're right, and that suits me just fine," he said. He spotted his dropped blanket and recovered it, wrapping it around his head as much to stanch the flow of blood as for warmth.

Maybe it was the loss of blood affecting his senses, or his recent exertion, or maybe the ravine blocked the wind, or maybe it was something else, but right now he didn't feel the cold quite as much as he had.

"Are you all right?" Ligacheva asked.

"I'm fine," Schaefer said. "You mentioned this boy's pals," he said. He parodied a bow, then pointed down the canyon toward the alien ship's location. "Shall we take a little hike and give them the bad news?"

"Yes," Ligacheva said. "Let's do that."

She ejected the magazine from her AK-100, then picked up one that someone had dropped during the massacre. She rammed it into place, then looked around at the bodies of her men—or rather Yashin's men.

She stared at the dead monster again.

"Should we strip this one?" she asked. "Its equipment might be useful."

"If we knew how to use it," Schaefer said. "Sure, the science boys would love to have it, but let's pick it up on the way back, shall we? There might be booby traps, and I'd rather not worry about them until after we've had a look at whatever's around the bend here."

Ligacheva hesitated. She reached down toward the monstrous corpse.

The shoulder cannon swiveled toward her.

She froze, staring at the black tube. Carefully she pulled her hand away, preparing to fling herself sideways if the cannon fired.

The tube did not move again. She waited and watched, but it remained motionless.

She didn't know whether that final movement had been caused by some final twitch of the creature's body, or some unfinished task the device had been performing, or some sort of automatic protective system. She decided she didn't care—Schaefer was right, the body might be booby-trapped, and stripping it could wait.

She straightened up slowly, watching the black tube. It never moved.

She stepped back, away from the body, then turned to face Schaefer.

"Let's go," she said.

27

"General Mavis?" the aide said. "If I might have a word with you in private, sir?"

Mavis tore his gaze away from the video monitors and glowered at the aide, recognizing him as White House staff. He pointed down the hall. "My office," he said.

A moment later, as the aide closed the door, Mavis demanded, "What is it?"

"They know, General," the aide replied immediately. "The Russians know everything."

Mavis frowned. "What do you mean, 'everything'? Just what do they know?"

"I mean the president just received a private cable from the Russian president, telling him that they knew we'd sent in a team with orders to capture or destroy the alien ship. The Russians are pissed as hell; they're threatening war if we don't get our people out of there or order them to surrender."

"War?" The general snorted. "Those bastards can barely feed their own people or keep their tanks running, and they're going to take *us* on?"

"They still have most of their nuclear arsenal, sir," the aide pointed out.

"Yeah, with an anticipated seventy percent failure-on-launch rate, thanks to their manufacture and maintenance . . ."

"Which they allowed for in building the damn things. Even if only thirty percent get through . . ."

"That's thirty percent that *launch*."

"Still, sir, the throw weight . . ." The aide caught himself. "Why are we arguing this? With all due respect, sir, we don't want a war with the Russians in any case."

"And we aren't going to get one," Mavis retorted. "They get excited if someone says nasty words to the Serbs, or buys a Lithuanian tractor, but we haven't had a war yet, have we?" He sat on the edge of his desk. "So what did the president say about this cable?"

"Well, sir, he was ready to tough it out until some wonk from the DOD mentioned that it was General Philips and that cop Schaefer running the show over there. You know how he feels about Philips."

"And?"

"And he wants the mission terminated *now*."

The general stared at the aide for a long moment, then said, "Shit. Any wiggle room?"

"No, sir. Direct order."

"He knows what we're giving up here?"

"He knows, sir. He also remembers that crater

in Central America and figures the Russians aren't
going to come out of this looking any better than we
are."

"He's putting a lot of faith in how good these
things are at covering their tracks."

"Yes, sir, he is—but not without reason, given
the past record."

Mavis eyed the aide, but the aide didn't say anything more, didn't explain the statement. The lack
of further comment, and the aide's blank expression, made it plain that that was the end of *that*
topic.

Mavis sighed. "Are we in contact with Philips at
present?" he asked.

"Yes, sir," the aide said. "He's just now got his
satellite uplink in full operation in the radio room of
that pumping station."

The general nodded. "Figures. I'd hoped that
maybe he'd moved on to the primary site, and we
couldn't reach him to pull the plug, but no such
luck. Well, if he's there, give him a jingle and tell
him the show's closing out of town. He knows the
procedure for pickup."

"Yes, sir. Will that be all?"

"Unless you've got some more bad news for me,
yes, that's it. Thank you."

The aide turned and left, and General Mavis
stared moodily at the map of the world on one wall
of his office. He focused on the Yamal Peninsula, in
the middle of Russia's useless, icebound northern
coast.

"Too bad," he said to himself. "Invisibility,
spaceships, energy cannons—all those toys we can't
have . . . and it might have been real interesting to
go toe-to-toe with the Russkies and find out once

and for all who's top dog." He sighed and stood up. "I wonder who spilled the beans?"

Rasche ran a hand over the sleek leather upholstery.

He'd gotten over his brief feelings of disloyalty about dealing with the Russians—after all, his government was up to some pretty dirty tricks here—but he was still adjusting to the reality of being here, on the other side of the world, in the Russian heartland.

He had, up until now, bought into the usual media image of post-Soviet Russia, all those newspaper stories and TV reports about the collapsed economy, the organized crime, the hard times. He had thought that the Russians were all on the verge of starvation, begging in the streets for bread and using their worthless rubles for wallpaper to keep out their infamous winters.

Maybe *some* of them were hurting, he thought, but judging by this limo Ambassador Komarinets was doing just fine, and Moscow in general had looked pretty solid.

They weren't in Moscow now, though—they were pulling through the gate of some military installation in the back end of nowhere.

"I am afraid, Mr. Rasche, that from here on our transportation will not be so comfortable," the ambassador remarked.

Rasche resisted the temptation to remark that the fourteen-hour flight on Aeroflot hadn't exactly been luxurious, and the military transport that got them from Moscow to wherever the hell they were now had been a flying Frigidaire. The limos, in

Moscow and again here, had been a welcome change.

He should have known it wouldn't last.

"I don't want to sound like a whiner, Ambassador," he said, "but are we almost there?"

Komarinets smiled. "You don't sound like a whiner, Mr. Rasche," he said. "You just sound like an American—spoiled and impatient. At least you Americans understand long distances, not like most of the Europeans, all jammed together in their little countries." He offered a cigarette, which Rasche refused with a gesture.

"To answer your question," the ambassador said as he snapped his cigarette case closed and tucked it back into his coat, "yes, we are almost there. From here, though, there are no roads open at this time of year, so we must take a vehicle that can travel on snow." He waved at the tinted car window behind him, and Rasche saw a line of ugly military-green vehicles standing beside the limo as it slowed to a stop.

They looked like a god-awful hybrid of snowmobile and semi, but Rasche supposed they'd do the job. A group of soldiers was standing, waiting, beside one of the tractor things; from their attitudes, Rasche guessed that the plump one in the middle was some sort of big shot.

A soldier opened the limo door and Rasche climbed out; the ambassador was doing the same on the other side. Komarinets spoke to the plump officer, but Rasche couldn't make out a word; he'd never had any gift for languages, and had never tried learning Russian in the first place. He remembered a few words of high school French and some choice phrases of gutter Spanish he'd picked up on the streets of the Big Apple, but that was about the full extent of his linguistic prowess outside his native English.

He stood and shivered while the Russians talked.

After a moment's conversation the ambassador turned to Rasche.

"This is General Ponomarenko," he said. "This entire military district is under his command, and he personally selected the officer in charge of operations at the site, a Lieutenant Ligacheva."

"I regret to say that that is correct," the general added, speaking slowly and with a heavy accent. "Her performance has been a disappointment. I look forward to relieving her of her command as soon as we locate her." He gestured at one of the snow tractors; as he did the engine started with a roar, making further conversation impractical.

"Come, we board now," Ponomarenko shouted, holding open the tractor door.

Rasche shrugged and climbed aboard.

28

Schaefer paused, balanced atop a ten-foot slab of rock, and looked back at Ligacheva, with his "borrowed" AK-100 held easily in one hand. She was moving slowly, creeping across the rocks. "We have to keep moving," he called. "As soon as those things figure out that we killed their sentry, they'll be coming after us!"

"Keep moving," Ligacheva repeated, nodding as she shifted her own weapon to the other hand so that she could better steady herself against the rock wall. "Ah. This must be what you Americans call a 'strategy.' Very good."

Schaefer smiled slightly, then looked around at the icy walls of the canyon.

Another reason he had wanted to keep moving was so he wouldn't freeze to death; his fancy plastic suit was less and less use with each step, as more of the insulating fluid leaked out, and he'd lost more blood than he liked. The blanket wrapped around his head was stiff with blood; he was pretty sure the flow had stopped, but if he'd been safe at home he knew he'd be in bed—or a hospital!—resting and recovering.

He sure wouldn't be out here in subzero weather.

Ligacheva had her heavy overcoat and fur hat, so maybe the cold wasn't such a problem for her.

He paused, noticing something.

Was it really a problem for either of them? The air didn't have the same vicious numbing bite to it that it had had before. True, the canyon walls shut out the wind, but . . .

"Is it my imagination, or is it warming up out here?" he said.

Ligacheva glanced at him. "Why do you ask?"

"Because the ice ahead looks like it's *melting,*" Schaefer said. "And unless I'm hallucinating from loss of blood, I hear water dripping somewhere. It's midwinter, this is Siberia—ice melting?"

"Indeed," Ligacheva said, staring. "And beyond that, the ground is bare." She pointed.

Schaefer looked at the area the Russian indicated and saw earth that was not just uncovered, but torn up and raw. "Something tells me that's not shown on your friend's map," he said.

"Your something speaks the truth," Ligacheva agreed. She watched as the American trudged ahead.

Schaefer was an enigma to her. He was endlessly bitter and cynical, constantly mocking any sort of authority, loyalty, trust, even simple humanity—yet he was *here,* pushing on into the unknown against a fearsome foe. He had fought the alien sentry with little more than his bare hands—and for what? He professed no love for his fellow man, no devotion to his homeland. The other Americans plainly hated him, he had mentioned no family or friends . . .

Perhaps his life was so empty that he had no fear of losing it. He seemed to exist in a friendless world of pain and death; perhaps those devils from the stars were all he had left to give his existence meaning or purpose.

"It's warm," Ligacheva said, removing her hat and shoving it into a pocket.

"It's more than warm," Schaefer replied, unclipping the collar of his plastic suit. "Something's got the temperature way up—it must be pushing sixty degrees . . ."

"*Sixty?*" Ligacheva exclaimed. Then she realized that the American must be using the foolish, archaic Fahrenheit scale, and quickly worked the conversion in her head. Fifteen or sixteen degrees Celsius—yes, that was about right. She unbuttoned her coat as Schaefer unzipped.

They were walking on bare, moist stone now, without even lingering traces of ice. Something had not just melted the ice and snow, but had boiled most of it away, heating the canyon air in the process.

"What could possibly produce so much heat?" she wondered aloud.

Schaefer, in the lead and scrambling up onto a boulder just at a bend in the ravine, stopped in his tracks and pointed around the corner.

"How about that?" he asked.

She stepped up on the boulder beside him, to where she could see around the corner, and she, too, stopped dead.

They had, beyond question, found the alien ship.

It lay in a pit ahead of them; the heat it radiated had melted the permafrost, and its weight had let it sink down into the formerly frozen mud that lined the bottom of the canyon. It was half-buried in dirt, mud, and gravel.

It was gigantic. It was an immense mass of *something*, but neither Ligacheva nor Schaefer could decide, upon looking at it, whether it was metal or some other material entirely—to Ligacheva it looked almost like bone. Its shape was curving, organic, impossible to describe. Large parts of its surface were an eerie red that seemed to glow dully in the darkness of the arctic night; the rest was lost in shadows, black against that luminescent crimson.

And one arched area, roughly the size and shape of a large door, glowed a brighter red and appeared to be an opening into the ship's interior.

"I think it's a different model from the ones I saw in New York," Schaefer said. "Can't be sure, as I didn't get a look at those from above like this."

"Is that . . . that opening, there . . ." Ligacheva struggled to phrase the question she wanted to ask.

"Looks like the welcome mat's out," the American said, answering her.

"Should we go in?" Ligacheva asked.

Schaefer hesitated, considering his answer—and saw the air shimmer slightly just beside the opening. The shimmer seemed to move away, across the hull—then the rock blocked his view and he lost sight of it.

It could have been that dizziness from loss of blood had made him imagine it, but Schaefer didn't think so. He thought it was real.

"No need to hurry," he said, stepping back down off the boulder. He ducked back out of sight and settled comfortably onto a rock.

If that shimmer had been an alien, and it had already seen him, they were as good as dead—but he was hoping it hadn't seen him.

Ligacheva joined him behind the bend in the canyon wall and looked at him, puzzled.

"Now what?" she asked.

"Quiet," he said. "And try not to move. I thought I spotted one of those things."

Ligacheva tensed; the two of them sat motionless in their sheltered corner for a long moment.

Schaefer was just beginning to decide that he had imagined that shimmer after all when he saw it again, moving along the far wall of the canyon. He watched.

Ligacheva saw the American's eyes focus on something across the ravine; she turned her own head and searched, but couldn't spot it.

Then it was gone, and Schaefer relaxed.

"I think our boy's gone to check on his buddy up the canyon," he said.

"The sentry we killed?"

Schaefer nodded.

"Then it will know we are in the area," Ligacheva said. "What will it do?"

"That's a very good question," Schaefer said. "And figuring out an equally good answer is why I'm sitting here trying to think."

He looked around, studying their surroundings—which were almost entirely bare rock. This entire stretch of the ravine had been cooked free of ice. "That thing's radiating an unbelievable amount of heat," he said. "That would explain why the satellites picked it up on infrared."

Ligacheva nodded. "We knew this," she said.

"But when those boys stopped by the Big Apple to play last year, we couldn't spot them with infrared," Schaefer pointed out. "We couldn't spot them with much of anything. They've got stealth technology that makes a B-2 bomber look like a fucking Goodyear blimp wrapped in neon."

"Then I would say that something must be broken in there," Ligacheva said. "This ship is hardly invisible."

"That's another thing," Schaefer said. "The ships that cruised Third Avenue *were* invisible, but we can see this baby just fine. I'd say a *lot* of things must be pretty broken up in there."

Ligacheva nodded. She gestured at the sides of the ravine, where the rock had been broken and scarred by some recent impact. "As you said earlier, I do not think they intended to land here at all, and from the appearance of this place, I do not think they landed well."

Schaefer nodded. "That's right—it's pretty clear that this wasn't a planned visit. That might explain part of their attitude problem—it must have been a rough ride bouncing down this canyon."

"Understanding their ill temper does not tell us how to deal with it."

"Oh, I don't know," Schaefer said. "Knowing that they're pissed at the whole damned universe gives us a clue that they aren't going to want to listen when we ask them nicely to surrender."

Ligacheva frowned. "If you actually saw one of them just now . . ." she began.

"Oh, I saw it, Schaefer said. "And I'm glad it didn't see us."

"When it finds its dead companion, it will return here," Ligacheva pointed out. "It will then be angry at *us,* as well as the universe, no?"

"Could be," Schaefer conceded.

"And while it did not detect us this time, we cannot count on being so fortunate a second time."

"Yeah, I'd thought of that."

"We must act quickly then, before it returns."

"Act how? What would you suggest we do?"

Ligacheva's mouth opened, then closed again.

"I don't know," she admitted.

"Neither do I," Schaefer said. He dumped the pack from his shoulder. "I think it's time to check out just what General Philips and his high-tech boys packed us for lunch; maybe there's something here that will give us an idea. After all, the general got all this fancy equipment to deal with that ship down there—maybe some of it'll actually work. I've lugged this stuff all this way on the off chance we'll need it, so let's see what Lynch handed me to carry." He opened the pack's top flap and reached in.

Most of the pack was filled with solid chunks of something heavy. Schaefer pulled out a few and inspected them, then poked at the gadgets underneath.

"C-4," Schaefer said. "Demolitions grade. And detonators, timers, impact fuses . . . we've got a whole wrecking crew here. Tasty stuff."

"Useful against *that*?" Ligacheva said, pointing at the alien ship.

"If it were detonated in the right place, yes," Schaefer said thoughtfully. "At least, if their vehicles are anything like ours, and not completely invulnerable." He reached into the pack again and brought out several ammo clips. He hefted them, feeling their weight, and read the label on one.

"Teflon-coated," he said. "Depleted uranium shells, magnum charge. These things ought to punch through steel plate as if it were cheese." He fitted one magazine to the AK-100. "And interchangeable," he said. "Smithers and Lynch and the rest may be a bunch of assholes, but the general's tech boys think of everything."

"The Kalashnikov Design Bureau, you mean," Ligacheva said. "The AK-100 was designed to accept almost any standard light round."

"These things may be small caliber, but they aren't *light*," Schaefer said. "We'll let everyone share the credit, shall we?" He turned the pack over to be sure he hadn't missed anything, then looked at the booty he had spread on the rock. "Now, what can we do with it all?"

Ligacheva looked around.

"The permafrost is melting," she said. "That's what holds this place together—the ice. If you planted some of your explosives in the canyon wall, you might be able to bring the whole thing down on top of them."

Schaefer looked up and around at the rocks. He stuffed the explosives back into the pack, slipped the AK-100 onto his shoulder, then stepped back up on the boulder overlooking the downed ship.

Ligacheva stepped up beside him.

"You think the rocks are . . ." Schaefer began, leaning forward for a better view.

He didn't finish the sentence. The boulder abruptly gave way beneath them.

Together, man, woman, and rock tumbled down the side of the pit and slammed heavily onto the top of the spaceship, landing with a resounding crash. A full-blown avalanche followed them immediately, showering stone and debris onto the hot surface of the ship.

Schaefer landed flat on his back, then slowly sat up. His plastic jumpsuit pulled away from the hot metal only reluctantly, leaving an oval of sizzling goo—the outer layer of the plastic had melted away.

Ligacheva had landed on her side and had climbed quickly back atop the fallen boulder, burning the palm of one hand in the process and scorching a long streak of black onto her overcoat. The ship was *hot*.

Schaefer joined her atop the rock before the rest of his suit could melt away, and the two of them crouched there, staring at the opening into the ship's interior, scarcely a dozen meters away.

"Do you think anyone heard that?" Ligacheva asked.

"You could have been front row center at a Who concert and heard that," Schaefer said. "If there's anyone still aboard, let's just hope they're too damn busy with repairing everything that's busted in there to come check out another rockslide." He pointed at a few scattered rocks that had apparently fallen onto the ship earlier as the ice had melted. Then he hefted the pack that he had somehow managed to hang on to and scanned the sides of the ravine.

He didn't see any suspicious shimmer, but that didn't mean much—it was dark up there.

It was light inside the ship, though—the red glow was almost alluring from this angle. And if that one he had spotted was the only one left, if there had only been two aboard this ship, then right now the ship was deserted.

Even if there were others aboard, they *might* be too busy with repairs to notice intruders. They certainly wouldn't *expect* intruders—walking straight into the enemy's home would surely seem insane to them.

Hell, it probably *was* insane, but that didn't bother Schaefer at all.

"As long as we're on their front porch," he said, "let's drop in."

Ligacheva turned to stare at him. Schaefer hefted the pack full of C-4.

"And while we're in there," he said, "we'll give them a little something to remember us by."

29

He must be here someplace," Kurkin said as he peered down an empty corridor, his AK-100 at the ready. His breath formed a thick cloud in the cold air, and he suppressed a shiver. "He wasn't with the others, and we didn't find any tracks in the snow . . ."

"This is mad," Afanasiev said as he swung his own weapon about warily. "He could be anywhere in the entire complex! How can so few of us hope to search it all without letting him slip past us? Especially when one of us must guard the other Americans!"

"And what would you have us do instead?" Kurkin asked sarcastically.

"Let him go!" Afanasiev said. "He is only one old man—what can he do?"

"One man with a weapon can do quite

enough . . ." Kurkin began. Then he stopped. "Listen!" he whispered.

Afanasiev stopped and listened. "Voices," he said. "But . . . do I hear *two* voices?"

"The radio room," Kurkin said. "He's in the radio room, and he has contacted his people—perhaps with his own satellite link, perhaps with our equipment. That's the other voice you hear."

Afanasiev frowned thoughtfully. "That room has only one door, yes?"

Kurkin nodded.

"We have him trapped, then."

"Let us take no chances," Kurkin said. "I have had enough of these damned Americans and their tricks. I say we go in shooting."

Afanasiev considered that, then nodded. "I have no objection," he said.

"On my signal, then."

Together they crept up toward the radio-room door, AK-100s at the ready. The voice from the radio grew louder as they approached.

". . . read you, Cold War One, and acknowledge your situation. We reiterate, new orders per Cencom, the mission has been scrubbed, repeat, *scrubbed*. Over."

Kurkin's rusty schoolbook English wasn't enough to make sense of any of that—he could only pick out about one word in three with any certainty.

He hoped that whatever the voice was saying wasn't of any real importance to anyone.

The radio voice stopped, and the trapped American didn't reply—he was undoubtedly, Kurkin thought, considering his answer.

The silence was unacceptable, though—if they

waited, the American might hear their breath or the rustle of clothing. Kurkin waved.

The two of them swung around the door frame, weapons firing in short bursts as they had been taught. A dozen slugs smacked the concrete walls, sending chips and dust flying in all directions.

Then they stopped shooting as they both realized they had no target. The radio room was empty. The radio was on, and a metal case stood open on a table with wires and a small dish antenna projecting from it—the American's satellite uplink, obviously.

The American wasn't there.

"Where is he?" Afanasiev asked, baffled. He stepped into the room.

The open door swung around hard and slammed into him, knocking him off his feet, and before Kurkin could react, he found himself staring at the muzzle of an M-16. He had lowered his own weapon and could not bring it up in time.

He couldn't understand what the American said, but the situation was clear enough. He carefully placed his AK-100 on the floor, then stood up again, hands raised.

Afanasiev, on the floor, turned and sat up—and saw the man with the M-16. He put down his AK-100 as well.

"You boys are noisy," General Philips remarked. "I heard you coming a hundred yards away. Took you long enough to get here." He kicked the AK-100s away, then looked over his two prisoners. He frowned.

"Ordinarily," he said, "I wouldn't do this to unarmed men, but you *did* come in with guns blazing." He flipped the M-16 around and smashed the butt against the standing Russian's temple.

Kurkin dropped.

Afanasiev cringed, and Philips paused. He took pity on the man and settled for tying him up, using a rifle strap to bind his wrists and a glove held in place with the helmet's chin strap as a make-shift gag.

Then he turned back to the radio.

"Cold War to base," he said. "Sorry about the interruption. Please repeat last message."

"Base to Cold War," the radio said. "There have been major changes in the operational dynamic. NORAD has tracked a special Russian transport on approach to your position; intelligence sources place a high-ranking political official on board. Further, Moscow has threatened full-scale military retaliation if there is any incident on Russian soil that violates their national security. The secrecy of the mission has been compromised."

"Shit," Philips said.

"You are hereby instructed to gather your men, avoid further hostile contact with alien life-forms, and permit their vessel to depart without interference. We don't want the Russians to get their hands on that alien technology—better both sides lose it. Understood?"

"*Shit!*" Philips said, more forcefully.

"Say again, Cold War?"

"Understood," Philips said. "We pack up and get out and let the bastards go."

"Affirmative."

"And what if they don't leave?" Philips muttered to himself. "I guess we'll just have to wait and see." Aloud, he said, "Acknowledged. Cold War One out."

He shut down the transmitter, packed up the

equipment, picked up the two AK-100s, then waved a farewell to the two Russians. He figured the unconscious one would wake up before too much longer, and the bound one could work his way loose, but neither one was going to be an immediate threat.

Taking a lesson from the pair of them he moved as stealthily as he could the entire distance from the radio room to the maintenance area under the pipeline where his men were being held at gunpoint—their captors hadn't relied on walls and doors this time.

All the same, it wasn't hard for Philips to get the drop on the Russians; the guards had been watching their captives, not their backs.

"Freeze!" he shouted as he stepped out of the shadows with the M-16 at ready.

The Russian guards probably didn't understand the word, but they got the message and stood motionless as the Americans took their weapons. Everyone there was half-frozen already, and fighting spirit was in short supply.

Once the weapons had changed hands and it was settled who was once again in charge for the moment, Philips addressed his men.

"I've been in touch with Cencom," he began. "Our mission's been . . ." He stopped, blinked, then said, "Wait a minute. Where the hell is *Schaefer*?"

"Who *cares*?" Wilcox asked. "Let's toe-tag these alien geeks and get the hell *out* of here before we freeze our fucking *balls* off!"

"He split with that bitch lieutenant when the shit came down," Lynch said.

"*Damn* him!" Philips growled. He chewed his lip, considering, for a few seconds, then announced,

"Look, we have new orders. The cat's out of the bag—someone let the Russkies know we're here, and we're shifting to CYA mode. Some kind of Russian big shot is coming up here for a look-see, and Cencom doesn't want him to find us. We've been instructed to abandon our mission and hightail it home without engaging either Russian or extra-terrestrial fire. Well, if I know Schaefer, he's out there kicking alien butt, and he isn't going to quit just because we tell him to. We need to *stop* him before he starts World War III."

"Who the hell's going to fight a war over a cop killing spacemen?" Lassen protested.

"Nobody," Philips said. "But if he leaves an abandoned starship sitting out there on Russian soil, there'll be one hell of a war over who gets to *keep* it. Now, come on, all of you! We'll leave these boys tied up to give us a lead, and then head out and see if we can stop Schaefer before he does any more damage."

Rasche looked out at the Siberian wilderness as the snow tractor plowed on through the darkness. He reached up and touched the window glass.

It was cold as hell out there; even with the heater on full blast, stinking up the cabin with engine fumes, the glass was so cold his fingertips burned where they touched it. Rasche was no hothouse flower, no California beachboy; he'd lived through a few subzero winters when the wind tore through the concrete canyons of New York like the bite of death itself. This, though—this cold was a whole new level of intensity.

Even worse than the cold, though, was the sheer desolation. The surface of the moon couldn't have been any deader than the landscape beyond the glass. Rasche was a city boy, born and bred; until he'd moved out to Bluecreek his idea of roughing it had been driving through a town that didn't have a 7-Eleven. He knew he wasn't any sort of wilderness scout, but this place . . . this was the end of the Earth. This was the end of life and hope and light made manifest. It was hard to imagine anything surviving out there.

Even Schaefer.

Then one of the Russians patted his shoulder and pointed, and Rasche squinted through the fog on the windows, trying to see what the man was indicating.

There was some sort of structure ahead.

"The Assyma Pipeline," Komarinets said. "We are almost to the pumping station."

There was a sudden burst of noise from the front seat, the two men there babbling excitedly in Russian and pointing to somewhere ahead.

"What is it?" Rasche asked, tensing. He was uncomfortably aware that he was unarmed; he had left his familiar .38 behind at the ambassador's request, to avoid any international incidents. If those *things,* those hunters from the stars, were out there somewhere . . .

"The driver thought he saw something moving up ahead, on the horizon," Komarinets explained.

"The aliens?" Rasche asked.

Then he remembered. They wouldn't *see* anything if the aliens were out there. The aliens were invisible when they wanted to be.

At least, assuming their gadgets worked in weather this cold, they were invisible.

Komarinets shook his head. "I think he imag-

ined it, or perhaps some bit of scrap paper or old
rag was blowing in the wind."

That statement, intended to reassure him,
made Rasche far more nervous—perhaps those
things *were* out there, but hadn't activated their
invincibility gadgets until they noticed the approaching convoy.

"Whatever he saw, there is nothing out there
now," Komarinets said.

"I hope so," Rasche said with heartfelt fervor. "I
really hope so."

30

Schaefer took a cautious step onto the ship's hull. "Warm," he said, "but my boots seem to be holding up."

"You told me they like the heat," Ligacheva said.

"So I did," Schaefer said, taking another step. "Didn't know that included their ships. You know, the hull feels almost *alive*."

"Maybe it is alive," Ligacheva suggested. "We don't know anything about it."

"So if we go in there, we'd be walking down its throat?" Schaefer grimaced. "I can think of a few things I'd like to ram down *their* throats."

"You want to make it warm enough for them, eh?" Ligacheva laughed nervously. "Well, why not?" She slid down off the boulder and began marching toward the opening, her AK-100 at the ready.

Schaefer smiled after her. "Why not?" he asked no one in particular.

Together, they walked into the ship.

Schaefer had expected some sort of airlock or antechamber between the opening and the ship's actual interior, but there didn't seem to be any; instead, they simply walked in, as if the opening were the mouth of a cave.

Once they were inside, though, the environment abruptly changed. The air stank, a heavy, oily smell, and was thick with warm fog, reducing visibility and making it hard to breathe. The light was a dull orange-red glow that came from the red walls, walls that were completely covered in elaborate, incomprehensible patterns. Whether those patterns were machinery, or decoration, or something structural, neither Schaefer nor Ligacheva could guess.

Whatever the patterns were, they were ugly. Schaefer didn't care to study them closely. He felt sick and dizzy enough already.

He wondered whether there were forcefields or some other device that kept the foul air in, or whether it just didn't *want* to mix with Earth's atmosphere.

"It's FM," he said in English, remembering something an engineer had once told him. "Fucking magic." He looked around at the ghastly light, the oozing, roiling fog of an atmosphere, the insanely patterned walls. He peered ahead to where the curving corridor opened out into a large chamber; patterned red pillars joined floor to ceiling, while other curving passages or rounded bays opened off every side. The place was a maze, all of it awash in baleful red light and stinking mist.

"No wonder they're such jerks," he said. "If I

spent fifteen minutes tooling around in a madhouse like this, I'd want to kill something myself." He hefted his AK-100. "In fact, I *do*."

"Wait," Ligacheva said. "Look over there."

"What?" Schaefer asked.

Ligacheva pointed at one of the rounded bays. Schaefer followed her as she led the way into it.

He saw, then, what had caught her eye. One section of wall here was not entirely red. It was hard to be sure, in the hideous red light, whether the pieces they were looking at were green or gray or black, but they weren't red.

The original red wall was torn open here; to Schaefer it looked as if something had exploded, but he supposed it might simply have been ripped apart by the aliens in their efforts at repair.

And parts of the pattern had been replaced, not with more of the red substance, but with ordinary pipes and valves and circuit boards. Schaefer could see Cyrillic lettering on several of them.

"Those filthy bastards," Ligacheva said. "The attack on the refinery, the workers slaughtered, my squad, my friends, all of them killed for *this*?"

"Got to give them credit," Schaefer said calmly. "They're resourceful. Something blew out here in the crash, or maybe *caused* the crash, and they needed to make an unscheduled pit stop. Your little pumping station served as their version of Trak Auto."

"But they *killed* all those men for a few pieces of *machinery*!" Ligacheva shouted. "It's not even anything secret, anything special—just plumbing! They could have *asked*! They could have bartered! They could have just *taken* it without killing—we couldn't have stopped them, and why would we care about *junk*?" She slammed the butt of her rifle against the pipes. "It's just *junk*!"

Schaefer grabbed her around the waist and pulled her back. "Stop it!" he ordered. "Damn it, that's enough!"

She struggled in his grip. "But . . ."

"Just shut up! There may be more of them aboard! If you want us to have a chance to do any good here, shut up before any of those things hear us!"

Ligacheva quieted, and Schaefer released her.

"Now, I admit," he said, "that our friends here have not been on their best behavior during their visit to your country. I agree completely that before we leave their ship, we should make sure to leave them a little something to remember us by."

"What sort of something?" Ligacheva demanded.

Schaefer hefted the pack. "Oh, a few of these toys in the right places ought to do wonders."

Ligacheva stared at the pack for a moment, then turned to the makeshift repair job.

"Yes," she said. "But . . ."

Before she could say any more, a blow from nowhere knocked both of them down. The choking mist seemed to be thicker down at floor level, and Schaefer was coughing even before the alien appeared out of nowhere and picked him up, one-handed, by the throat.

It was as big and ugly as any of the others Schaefer had ever seen. It wore no mask—presumably it had no need for one here aboard its own ship. Its yellow fingers and black claws closed on Schaefer's neck, not tight enough to inflict serious damage, but tightly enough that it lifted him easily and inescapably.

Ligacheva came up out of the fog with her AK-100 in hand, but before she could squeeze the trigger, in the second she took to be sure she wouldn't hit Schaefer, the monster slapped her back with its free hand. She slammed against the wall and slumped, dazed, back down into the mist.

Schaefer struggled in the thing's grip, but resisted the temptation to pry at its fingers. He *knew* these things were too strong for such a maneuver to do any good; strong as he was by human standards, he wouldn't be able to free himself. He needed to find another way to fight back. Bare-handed, he couldn't do anything; his AK-100 was out of reach; he needed some other weapon.

He reached back behind himself, stretching.

The creature growled at him, a grating, unearthly noise. The fingerlike outer fangs around its mouth flexed horribly, and the vertical slit of its mouth opened wide, revealing its inner teeth.

"Damn you to hell," Schaefer said as his hands closed on a shard of the shattered red wall of the spaceship's interior. He gripped it, felt the razor-sharp edge where it had broken, and yanked at it.

It came away in his hand, and without a second's hesitation he plunged it into the alien predator's side.

The creature screamed in pain and flung him aside as if he were so much junk mail, tearing the makeshift dagger from his grasp.

Schaefer rolled when he landed and came up gasping but intact. He started for the broken section of wall, hoping to find another sharp fragment he could use.

"Just tell me," he said as he watched the bellowing alien, looking for a chance to dodge past it toward the wreckage, "why Earth? Why is it always Earth? What's wrong with the big game on Mars, or Jupiter, or the goddamn Dog Star, or whatever the hell is out there? It's a big fucking galaxy, isn't it? Why can't you just . . ."

Then he saw the shadow in the fog behind his foe, and even before the new arrival turned off its invisibility shield, Schaefer knew he was facing a second enemy in addition to the wounded one.

Then the creature appeared, and Schaefer saw that it was carrying a corpse draped over its right shoulder—an alien corpse, the corpse of the sentry he and Ligacheva had killed out in the canyon.

"Oh, shit."

He backed up against the broken section of wall, knowing that he was letting himself be cornered, but not knowing what else he could do. The wounded predator was staggering slightly, holding its side, but still upright; the new arrival was ignoring its injured companion and staring directly at Schaefer, but not yet moving to attack. It lifted its dead companion off its shoulder and lowered the body gently to the floor, all the while keeping its masked eyes directed straight at Schaefer.

Then the uninjured alien reached up and disconnected something from its mask; gas hissed for a few seconds. It lifted the metal mask away and revealed its ghastly face; those hideous mouth parts, looking like some unholy hybrid of fang, finger, and tentacle, were flexing in anticipation. It took a step closer to Schaefer as he groped unsuccessfully for another sharp piece of wreckage.

Then Ligacheva came up out of the reeking mist again, her AK-100 at her shoulder, and fired.

The aliens, Schaefer knew, could shrug off

most small-caliber bullets; their hides were incredibly tough. Depleted uranium coated in Teflon, however, was something new to them; Ligacheva's shots punched through the monsters as if they were merely human, and glowing yellow-green blood sprayed from a dozen sudden wounds.

The previously unharmed creature went down at once; the fog swirled up in clouds. The other alien, presumably already heavily dosed with whatever these things used as the equivalent of endorphins, snapped its jagged double wrist blades into place and tottered several steps toward Ligacheva before collapsing into the mist.

"They aren't dead!" Schaefer shouted. He had seen before how tough these things were.

"I know that," Ligacheva said, irritated. She stepped forward, pointed the AK-100 at one alien's head, and squeezed the trigger.

Yellow gore sprayed.

She turned her attention to the other alien; it managed to roll over and raise one clawed hand as she approached, but that only meant that it took her last eight rounds directly in the face.

The echoes of the gunfire were oddly muffled in the foggy atmosphere and died away quickly.

Ligacheva stood over the three creatures—the two she had just taken down and the one she had slain earlier. She stared down at them through the mist, getting as good a look as she could at their ruined faces.

"*Now* they're dead," she said, satisfied.

"Probably," Schaefer agreed. "Let's not hang around to be sure, though. If there are any more of these joyboys aboard this madhouse, they could be here any minute."

"I can reload while you make your bomb . . ."

"I think we'd be smarter doing that outside," Schaefer said. "They could be here *now*—remember their little invisibility trick."

Something hissed somewhere. Ligacheva hesitated another half second, then turned and sprinted back up the corridor they had entered by.

Schaefer was right behind her.

A moment later they emerged into open air— *Earth's* air. Even the cool, flavorless Siberian air, utterly devoid of any scent of life, was far better than the stuff they had been breathing aboard the alien ship, and once they had scrambled from the hot hull up onto the familiar boulder they both paused for a few seconds to savor it.

Schaefer glanced at Ligacheva. She wasn't beautiful, but right then he was glad to be looking at her. "Pretty good shooting in there, comrade," he said.

"Credit your American technology," Ligacheva said. "And of course, my damned good aim." She ejected the spent magazine from her AK-100. "And give me another clip of that technology, would you?"

Schaefer smiled and opened the pack. He handed her another clip, then started pulling out blocks of C-4 and plugging in wires.

"If we wire this all into a single charge and put it back down inside there, it ought to tear their ship up just fine," he remarked as he worked.

"And we can scavenge the wreckage, and our governments can fight over it," Ligacheva said.

Schaefer shrugged as he wired a detonator into the series of charges. "I don't give a shit about that," he said. "I just want to make it plain to these bastards once and for all that Earth isn't a safe place to play."

Ligacheva didn't answer; she watched thoughtfully as Schaefer finished assembling his bomb and stuffed it back into his pack.

"Perhaps we should think about this a little further," she said at last as he strapped an electronic timer into place on top.

He looked up at her.

"I want them to pay for their crimes, too," Ligacheva said. "But I do not want American missiles to make sure my country does not use this starship to restore us to our former place as a world power."

"Washington hasn't got the guts to nuke anyone," Schaefer said. "We'll just steal it from you, and then everybody'll have it."

"And would that be a good thing?"

Schaefer started to answer, then froze. He was crouched on the boulder, the pack-turned-satchel-charge in one hand, facing the opening into the ship's interior.

Ligacheva whirled.

One of the alien monsters stood in the opening, looking out at them. It was visible and unmasked—it hadn't come out to fight, Ligacheva realized, but only to see what the hell was going on.

That didn't mean it wouldn't kill them both, given half a chance. It must know that they had killed its companions; she was suddenly horribly aware of the AK-100 she still held in her hands, the very gun that had blown the other monsters' heads apart.

If she shifted her grip to firing position and swung the weapon around, she might be able to shoot the alien—or it might take her own head off first. She had seen how fast those things could move, how fast they could kill.

She didn't try. She kept the gun pointed away. She looked at Schaefer to see whether he, too, was still frozen.

He wasn't. He was still working on his bomb.

"That's right," Schaefer called to the creature. "Come out and play! This C-4 will turn you into hamburger faster than UPN canceled *Legend*!"

Ligacheva turned to stare at Schaefer's fingers as he punched codes into his electronic detonator.

"But if you set it off now to kill that thing, the explosion will take us down with it!" she exclaimed.

Schaefer didn't look at her; he was staring at the alien, his attention focused entirely on his foe. "I'm tired of your games," he said. "I'm tired of *all* this crap! This time we're going to *finish* it . . ."

Ligacheva realized that he meant it, that he was ready and willing to die—he wanted only to give his death meaning, the meaning he seemed unable to find in life, by taking his foe with him.

She wanted to stop him, but he was too far away for her to reach the detonator in time, and even if she had been able to think of the words to shout, she knew he wouldn't have listened to her.

Then a shot rang out, and a bullet smacked off the starship's hull inches away from Schaefer's feet. Ligacheva, Schaefer, and the alien all turned simultaneously, looking for the source.

Five men in tan snowsuits stood on the rim of the ravine, looking down at them. A sixth man knelt, holding a smoking rifle.

"Drop it, cop, or the next one's right between your eyes! And drop your gun, too, Russkie!" the kneeling man called in English.

31

Schaefer stared at the man with the rifle. "Wilcox," he said. He lowered the pack gently to the boulder; it slid down onto the ship's hull.

"I'm sorry about this, son," General Philips shouted. "It's over!"

Ligacheva dropped her AK-100 and stared up at the men on the canyon rim. The Americans had tracked them from the pumping station, but they had not come to help against the monsters; instead they were *preventing* Schaefer from ending the alien threat.

It wasn't that they cared about Schaefer's life or Ligacheva's—the words of that man Wilcox had made that plain. It was . . . what? They wanted the alien alive? They wanted the ship?

Perhaps they simply didn't want the *Rodina*, the Motherland, to have the ship. They preferred that the alien fly away safely, to return and slaughter at whim.

Ligacheva began to understand just how Schaefer, the pampered American, had become as bitter as any Russian survivor of wars and revolutions and endless dark winters.

And what of the alien? Did it *want* to just fly away in its jury-rigged ship? She glanced at it.

It stood watching the men on the rim, watching and waiting, its hideously inhuman face unreadable. She wondered what it was thinking.

It hated the cold; it probably did want nothing but to leave.

"What's the story, General?" Schaefer called.

"You aren't going to like it," Philips called back. "And I don't like it any more than you do, but we've been ordered to let them lift off without interference. So back away, nice and easy."

Ligacheva wondered what the alien thought of all this. Did it understand the words? Was it confused? Did it think this was all some sort of trap?

Or was it just fascinated—or amused—by the spectacle of its prey fighting among itself?

"I've been dancing to your tune since this whole thing began, General," Schaefer said. "What the hell has it ever gotten me, listening to you? You people have taken everything that ever meant anything to me—my job, my home, my brother. What'll I get if I do what you tell me now—a bullet in the head? *Screw* it!"

Schaefer dove for the pack.

On the canyon rim Wilcox smiled coldly as he squeezed the trigger. "Been looking forward to this since that day on the firing range," he said as the rifle bucked in his hands. "Adios, cop!"

He had misjudged Schaefer's speed; the bullet tore through the flesh of Schaefer's outer thigh, nowhere near any vital organs.

It was enough to send Schaefer rolling out of control across the scorching-hot hull of the alien spaceship, though; he tumbled down past the pack and sprawled at the creature's feet, a yard from the open doorway.

He looked up at the thing, at the twitching mouth parts. He took a deep breath and smelled his own flesh starting to burn from the heat of the ship.

"Yeah, come on," he said to the creature. "Let's finish it!"

The monster looked down at him, its eyes narrowing, then glanced up at the canyon rim.

Then it turned and ran down into its ship, leaving Schaefer lying on the hull.

"No, you bastard!" Schaefer shouted after it. "You alien son of a bitch! Better I die fighting you than let that asshole Wilcox get me!" He tried to struggle to his feet and succeeded only in falling and rolling, this time tumbling clear off the side of the ship, landing in the gravel and mud that surrounded it.

"First shot was for God and country," Wilcox said, sighting in on Schaefer's head. "This one's for me!"

Beside him, General Philips clenched his teeth.

A rifle shot sounded, echoing from the walls of the ravine . . .

And Wilcox suddenly tumbled forward, blood running freely from the fresh wound where a bullet had punched through his shoulder.

Philips spun and looked uphill.

"And that one was for *me*," a voice called—a familiar voice with a bit of a Brooklyn twang.

Philips spotted the man with the smoking rifle—an overweight man in a Russian Army overcoat and fur-lined cap, carrying an AK-74. Somehow, despite the equipment, Philips had no doubt that the man was American.

"Howdy, General," the rifleman said. "Meet the *other* general." He waved with his free hand, and Philips saw another twenty or thirty men in Russian uniforms approaching, their rifles trained on the small band of Americans. One of them, a big man in an officer's coat, did not have a visible weapon, and the speaker gestured at him. "General Ponomarenko, of the Russian Army."

Ponomarenko stepped forward. "You men are trespassing!" he shouted in heavily accented English.

Below, standing on the boulder, Ligacheva listened and watched what little she could see from her place in the pit. She recognized Ponomarenko's voice and knew she ought to feel relieved that her people had come to the rescue, but instead she felt a wave of despair, the same sort of bitter despair that she thought the American detective must have felt. Right and wrong were being lost here; all that mattered was who had the drop on the other side, who had the weapons and where they were pointed. No one up there cared about the good men those things from the stars had slaughtered; all they cared about was political advantage. They didn't see the aliens as monsters, but as a potential technological treasure.

Her people—which is to say, all humanity, not merely Russians—were fighting among themselves while their true enemy killed with impunity and was allowed to escape.

What had so many died for? What had they suffered for? When this was over, what would anyone truly have gained?

Not justice, certainly.

She was suddenly distracted from the drama being played out above. The stone beneath her feet was starting to vibrate, and something was whining, a sound almost like a jet engine warming up.

She knew immediately what was happening and dove for the side, trying to get off the ship before it could launch. On her way she snatched up Schaefer's explosive-filled backpack—she didn't know why, but acted out of instinct.

The whining grew louder as she slid down beside Schaefer. He was struggling, trying to get to his feet, but his wounded leg wouldn't support him, and his burned flesh made any movement painful.

"They're getting ready to launch," he said.

"You think I don't know that?" she replied angrily. "Come on, we have to get clear!" She grabbed Schaefer's arm and threw it across her shoulders, and tried to heave them both up out of the pit the ship lay in.

She couldn't do it; Schaefer was too big, too heavy.

"Need a hand?" a voice said in English.

Ligacheva looked up and grasped the offered hand. Together, she and the stranger hauled Schaefer up across the rocks.

Schaefer, weak from burns and blood loss, looked up at their savior and said, "Rasche?"

"Yeah, it's me," Rasche replied. Ligacheva thought he sounded as if he were on the verge of tears. "For cryin' out loud, Schaef," the American said, "we've got to quit meeting like this!"

"Christ, Rasche," Schaefer asked, "how the hell did *you* get *here*?"

"I heard a few things and thought maybe you could use some help," Rasche said as he and Ligacheva pulled Schaefer farther up the side of the ravine. "Good friends are hard to find, y'know?"

Schaefer didn't answer. Ligacheva stared at him for a moment, then up at this Rasche.

Schaefer evidently wasn't as alone in the world as he had thought.

Ligacheva suddenly felt that she was intruding; once the three of them were safely off the steepest part of the slope, she left the American to his friend as the two men sought shelter in the rocky side of the canyon. They had found their peace for the moment, she thought. Schaefer had had his friend come for him, halfway around the world and through competing armies; even he could not find the universe completely bleak and without value in the face of such devotion.

For her own part Ligacheva had never doubted the existence of human warmth, even in the Siberian wastes. It was *justice* that she sought and that seemed so elusive, justice for the workers of Assyma who had been butchered by those things simply because they were in the way. She heaved Schaefer's backpack up and looked at the electronic detonator.

It seemed simple enough. She knew enough English to read the SET and START buttons, and of course numerals were the same in English and Russian.

Below her the rumbling and whining grew louder, rising in pitch.

She typed in 45—she couldn't have given a reason, but somehow forty-five seconds seemed right. She glanced down at the alien ship.

Openings at the stern were glowing blue, lighting the arctic night almost bright as day. The opening *she* cared about, though, the entrance to the ship's interior, was still a dull red—and still open, so far as she could tell.

She could throw the pack into it, she was sure. From where she stood, on a ledge on the canyon wall, it would be a long, difficult throw, but she could do it. She reached for the START button.

"That's quite enough, Lieutenant," General Ponomarenko's voice said from above.

She looked up at the muzzles of half a dozen rifles and Ponomarenko's unsmiling face.

"That is obviously an explosive of some sort," he said, "and you unquestionably intended to use it against that ship." He snorted. "I suspected your incompetence in Moscow, and now you've demonstrated it conclusively. You don't *destroy* this kind of power! Drop that device!"

Reluctantly Ligacheva obeyed, dropping the bomb to the ledge. She half hoped the ledge would crumble beneath her as the permafrost continued to melt, and that she and the bomb would tumble back onto the ship, where she could fling it into the opening before anyone could stop her.

The ledge remained solid.

Ponomarenko announced, "We hereby claim this trespassing alien vessel in the name of the Russian people!"

Ligacheva glanced at Schaefer. He was slumped on the rocks a dozen meters away, supported by his amazing friend Rasche, but he was watching her.

She thought he might say something to her, might offer her a few words of inspiration or encouragement, but all he did was smile.

The ground was shaking as the ship powered up.

"General, I don't think the pilot heard your claim," she said.

"The air force is on the way," Ponomarenko replied. "They will attempt to force it back down, should it launch. And if they fail—well, we will undoubtedly have other chances in the future."

"You think so?" Ligacheva said. She looked down at the ship, at the pack—she couldn't stoop down and throw it fast enough, not before those guns fired.

But she didn't have to throw it. She was no American, raised on their silly baseball and basketball. She was a Russian, and had spent every free hour of her childhood playing soccer.

"General," she said, "screw that!"

She turned, swung, tapped the START button with her toe as if setting a ball, then kicked hard in the most perfect, most important shot on goal she had ever made in all her years on the soccer field.

Despite the pack's utter failure to adhere to regulations regarding the weight or shape of the ball, it sailed neatly down into the opening, exactly where she wanted it, down through the starship's open door.

And then the whine turned into a roar and the world filled with blue-white fire as the starship finally launched itself up out of the mud and rock, out of the ravine, up into the arctic night.

32

Ligacheva blinked dust from her eyes and sat up, unsure how she had come to be lying on her back in the first place, unsure where she was.

She looked and saw that she was still on the rocky ledge in a Siberian ravine. Below her a hundred small fires lit the alien ship's launch trail; behind her, a dozen meters away, Schaefer and Rasche crouched amid the rocks, sheltering their heads from showering debris.

And far above, in the east, a speck of light was the departing starship.

Somehow she didn't think that the Russian Air Force was going to be able to catch it. Scarcely thirty seconds had passed since the launch, she was certain, and yet it was almost out of sight.

Thirty seconds . . .

Had the pack fallen out when the ship

launched? Had it penetrated far enough into the ship's interior to do any real damage?

And then the distant speck blossomed into a tiny fireball. The bomb had detonated . . .

And then the fireball exploded and lit the entire sky white in a tremendous blinding flash.

That was no C-4 explosion, she knew. The ship's power source, whatever it was, must have gone up—the C-4 must have done enough to set it off, or maybe the makeshift repairs had given way.

Whatever the cause, she was sure there would be no wreckage to analyze, no pieces to pick through and puzzle over, after such a blast.

She closed her eyes and waited for the after-image of the explosion to fade. When she opened them again, General Ponomarenko was looking down at her.

"Do you have any idea what you've *done,* you fool?" he bellowed at her. "Your military career is finished, Ligacheva! There will be a hearing, official inquiries, questions in parliament . . ."

"I'm looking forward to it," she retorted. "I welcome a chance to tell the world the way the new democratic Russia treats its soldiers and workers, and how we lied to the Americans about our visitors!"

"I'm sure that won't be necessary," a new voice said. An aristocratic civilian stepped up beside the general. He switched from Russian to English. "I'm Grigori Komarinets, Russia's ambassador to the United Nations. I think we can count on General Philips to cooperate in clearing up this little incident without involving parliament or the press. There's no need to worry the public with details—is there, General?"

Ligacheva didn't need to hear Philips's reply or any further conversation. She turned and spat, clearing dust from her face and bile from her heart.

Neither side would want to admit how far they had been willing to go to steal alien technology—or prevent the other side from doing so. Neither side would want to discuss the farcical, homicidal behavior displayed by Yashin, Wilcox, and the rest. And neither side wanted to admit that the aliens even existed.

So they would keep everything quiet. Philips and Komarinets would concoct a cover story— Iranian terrorists staging an incident, perhaps— and everyone would abide by it.

She, too, would stay silent about the truth, because if she did not her military career would be over, and she might well die suddenly in an "accident," or perhaps a "suicide" while despondent over the loss of her comrades.

And besides, no one would believe her. Alien monsters crash-landed in Siberia? Who could accept such a thing?

She smiled bitterly at Schaefer and his friend. They understood the truth; Schaefer had tried to tell her. They understood—but they carried on anyway.

A dozen yards away Rasche smiled back, then asked Schaefer, "What the hell was that all about? I heard the ambassador planning to hush it all up, but what were the girl and the general talking about?"

"He was threatening her, and she told him to go to hell," Schaefer translated. "Kid learns fast. If the

Russians don't want her anymore, maybe we can find a place for her on the NYPD."

Rasche snorted. "You'd do that to her? And here I thought you *liked* her!"

Schaefer smiled. "Funny thing, Rasche," he said. "I think I do."

ABOUT THE AUTHOR

NATHAN ARCHER was born and raised in New York City, and took a government job straight out of college. This didn't satisfy his creative urges, so he wrote, for his own amusement, in his spare time.

When budget cuts left him unemployed in 1992, he decided it wouldn't hurt to see if he could write for money.

Turns out he can. He's now the author of *Star Trek: Deep Space Nine #10: Valhalla, Star Trek: Voyager #3: Ragnarok,* and *Predator: Concrete Jungle,* with several other projects in the works.

Archer lives in Chicago and has no children or pets. His eyes are green, and other details are classified.